LETTERS
of
ENLIGHTENMENT

JEFFREY FAULKNER

WESTBOW°
PRESS
A DIVISION OF THOMAS NELSON
& ZONDERVAN

Scripture taken from the Holy Bible, NEW INTERNATIONAL VERSION®.
Copyright © 1973, 1978, 1984 by Biblica, Inc. All rights reserved worldwide.
Used by permission. NEW INTERNATIONAL VERSION® and NIV® are
registered trademarks of Biblica, Inc. Use of either trademark for the offering
of goods or services requires the prior written consent of Biblica US, Inc.

WestBow Press books may be ordered through booksellers or by contacting:

WestBow Press
A Division of Thomas Nelson & Zondervan
1663 Liberty Drive
Bloomington, IN 47403
www.westbowpress.com
1 (866) 928-1240

Because of the dynamic nature of the Internet, any web addresses or
links contained in this book may have changed since publication and
may no longer be valid. The views expressed in this work are solely those
of the author and do not necessarily reflect the views of the publisher,
and the publisher hereby disclaims any responsibility for them.

Any people depicted in stock imagery provided by Thinkstock are models,
and such images are being used for illustrative purposes only.
Certain stock imagery © Thinkstock.

ISBN: 978-1-4908-5979-8 (sc)
ISBN: 978-1-4908-5980-4 (hc)
ISBN: 978-1-4908-5978-1 (e)

Library of Congress Control Number: 2014920139

Printed in the United States of America.

WestBow Press rev. date: 11/20/2014

Written In Memory of Our Deceased Spouses,
Ruth and Gary

Acknowledgments

I would like to express my appreciation to my daughters, Kim and Kara, and my sons-in-law, Matt and Justin for their assistance with Letters of Enlightenment.

Contents

Preface

There we were, my wife and I, watching the nightly news, like we did so many times. This night was different. My wife got up and turned off the news in disgust over the violence, war, and depressing scenes. She looked at me and said, "We must do something to make a difference." What could a little couple from the Midwest do to change the world? "Let's write an inspirational letter to friends and family," she said.

And so began a journey of writing monthly letters to over sixty people. I wrote that first letter after a lot of praying to the Holy Spirit. Would you believe that the Holy Spirit and I have been writing a monthly good-news inspirational letter every month for the past ten years? These letters have taught me more about our loving God and have also enabled me to spread the Word to others.

My wife Ruthy died over five years ago after a five-year struggle with ovarian cancer. I loved her deeply, and she inspired me so very much. I was given another gift three years ago when I was married to Diane. She, too, lost a spouse—Gary—to cancer over seven years ago.

All our lives are strangely woven with patterns of joy and suffering. When we share our sufferings, struggles, joys, and dreams with others, our lives seem to make more sense.

One of the most difficult tasks in life is accepting our sufferings. We just want to run and hide from them. But suffering has its own clock, its own schedule.

My letters have taught me so much about suffering. They have helped me learn something new each time. When one loses a loved one, one goes through so much grieving, so much change, and so much uncertainty. Sometimes, one despairs, even reaching a "black hole" in life where nothing seems to matter. I am convinced that if we can hold on during our times of weakness, then our Lord will begin the process of strengthening us. I have tried to convey this message in many of my letters.

There are so many ways to minister to others in this world of ours. So many of our brothers and sisters are thirsting for the good news of the Lord.

We all have a purpose. We will all have to face our Lord someday. The question is, are we living a prayerful life, following Jesus, and doing His will?

Writing my monthly letters has brought me closer to the heart of Jesus. I hope that as you read this little collection of inspirational letters, they bring peace to you. May they give you pause and a time to reflect. May I leave you with just one thought? Always rely on Jesus. He loves you so much, no matter how difficult your life may be. You see, you are His very special child.

Jeffrey Faulkner

Prayer

April 1, 2005

Dear Friends,

Jesus was ready for His trial in life, death on a cross, because He prayed daily to the Father. The disciples were overcome with fear and distress because they could not stay awake and pray with the Lord. I pray each morning that the Lord will stay close to my heart and that I will do His will. Complete submission to God—that's what it is all about.

Sometimes, complete submission to God brings fear in our lives because we are afraid to give up those things that give us worldly pleasure. Life is about giving glory and praise to God and surrendering all to Him. Give God your fears, sufferings, joy, work, play, money—it all belongs to Him.

When we pray to God, we celebrate His uniqueness and His significance in our lives. We have so many opportunities to pray each day, and yet, sometimes, God becomes secondary to us. Prayer works. We all feel the power of prayer if we only put our trust in God.

The more we pray, the more our minds and hearts become centered on Christ. The world is in need of much prayer. You and I can help each other this very moment if we take time to pray for each other.

Prayers and peace,

Jeff and Ruth

Heaven

May 1, 2005

Dear Friends,

I recently read a book entitled *Where Heaven Begins* by Rosanne Bittner. It is about a single woman who undertakes a journey on foot from California to Alaska in the 1890s. She wants to meet up with her brother, who is the only family member she has left. Her journey is quite a struggle.

In the midst of our lives, do we really believe that heaven begins when we die? Or does God afford us glimpses of His magnificent reward right here on Earth?

I really believe that no matter how bad a day may be, we can always see a glimpse of heaven if we only open our eyes and hearts. Here are some of those glimpses of heaven that I appreciate:

- a smile from someone I do not know
- a spectacular sunset that only our God has the power to create
- a quiet place to meditate and give praise and glory to our God

- a newborn baby with all of its innocence
- two people of different faiths sharing the same good news of their belief in Jesus Christ
- taking the time to see the awesome beauty of a flower and becoming filled with joy because of God's wonderful creation
- holding hands in prayer and thanksgiving with another
- when the Holy Spirit fills our hearts with complete joy and love

What are your glimpses of heaven? Look for them each day. Our gracious Father has given us so much to see, and we only need to open our hearts to His many, many blessings.

Have a great spring, and may Jesus fill every day of your life with a glimpse of heaven.

Love and peace,

Jeff and Ruthy

Struggles

June 1, 2005

Dear Friends,

Sometimes, life's struggles are so overbearing that we can hardly stand them. We wonder, we think, we cry, we get angry, we overreact, and, in some instances, we feel like giving up.

Wow! What would we do without our faith? To what would you and I cling for hope? How could we even survive?

When Jesus left this world after dying for our sins and rising into heaven, He left His Spirit with us—the Holy Spirit. Each one of us has been filled with that Spirit and all the grace we need to overcome any obstacle or mountain we may encounter, if only we remember that the Spirit is alive within us.

Sometimes, we are afraid to profess our true beliefs and, therefore, conceal our faith. We may be too cautious about our faith and believe that it is not the appropriate time to reveal our feelings. We need to stand tall with our faith, let others know how we feel about our God, and let the Holy Spirit work within us. We need to showcase the Holy Spirit within us by loving all people and helping those who are less fortunate. But most of all, we need to remember that the Spirit dwells within each of us.

Observe one minute of silence each day, and let the Holy Spirit talk to you and pour His graces on you. You may not hear Him at that very moment, but He will be present in your heart and soul.

"But if by the spirit you put to death the misdeeds of the body, you will live because those who are led by the Spirit of God are sons and daughters of God" (Romans 8:13–14).

Love and peace,

Jeff and Ruthy

Enlarge My Territory

August 1, 2005

Dear Friends,

"Oh, that you would bless me indeed and enlarge my territory, that Your hand would be with me, and that You would keep me from evil, that I may not cause pain" (1 Chronicles 4:10)!

This verse is a prayer from a man named Jabez, who was bold enough to ask God for the things that God really wants to give us. Many of you have heard of the book *The Prayer of Jabez,* written by a wonderful man by the name of Bruce Wilkinson. His books are inspiring and uplifting.

Ruth and I began praying the prayer of Jabez several months ago. I believe that God really does bless us in many ways. I want to focus only on the second thought in this prayer, "Enlarge my territory." This is when you ask God to enlarge your life so you can make a greater impact for Him. We are expanding our ministry when we help bring others to a closer relationship with Jesus. It is a way of expressing our faith when we are at work or with a friend or stranger.

When was the last time you asked God to enlarge your territory? Reading and studying the Bible can help you understand how to do this. Sometimes, asking God for more to do can be frightening. You might be afraid to step outside of your comfort zone to help others. Ask God, and listen to Him. He speaks to all of us, but sometimes we don't take the time to listen. He talks to all of us. How? Through the Holy Scriptures of the Bible, the Word of God.

When you pray, God will send people into your life whom you can help. Just remember to keep your heart open to all the wonderful opportunities to help people of all walks of life. "Whatever you do to the least of my people, you do unto me" (Matthew 25:40).

God will always be beside you as you enlarge your territory. Take what God has entrusted to you and multiply it many times, and you will be doing God's will. The going may not always be easy, but the rewards will be great. God will always intervene when you put His agenda before yours.

Let us pray for each other as we explore the fantastic opportunities to help our brothers and sisters that God will shower on us. You are a very special person to God. He loves you very much, and so do we.

Love and peace,

Ruth and Jeff

Jeffrey Faulkner

God Promotion

September 1, 2005

Dear Friends,

We hope that all of you are in good health and doing fine. We recently read a book entitled *Turn* by Max Lucado. It is about change. We would like to share some thoughts with you about this powerful little book.

Turn from self-promotion to God promotion. We need to humble ourselves and pray. When we get up each day, we should ask how we can serve others, not what we can do for ourselves. To serve others, we must be at peace with ourselves. The wars being fought are struggles for peace. They are fought because people cannot live a peaceful life. The mentality is that fighting will solve the problem and bring victory/peace. What wars do we fight in our personal lives? Is there someone we need to forgive? Do we spend more time doing our own thing instead of serving others? How much time do we spend in prayer each day?

Sometimes, we need to make a turn in our lives. We need to go north instead of south. We need not be afraid. God is always near. Turn to

God. Turn to prayer. Turn to repentance. Today, I ask God to forgive me, a sinner. How do you feel about the way God is being treated today? His name is forbidden more and more. Don't be afraid to promote our God in public. If you don't, then no one will. We have so much in this country, and yet we are afraid to mention the name of God in public—the one who has given us everything we have. America exists by the power of God—not by our governing bodies. And yet we forget and remove the name of God from as many places as possible—schools, government buildings, and our homes. The Bible says, "If you ever forget the Lord your God and follow other gods, worshipping and bowing down to them, you will certainly be destroyed" (Deuteronomy 8:19), yet the world continues to worship false gods such as materialism, work, pornography, money, power, and laziness.

America exists to bless God, not for God to bless America. God can change nations that are bad. God is in control. But we need to pray—pray with all our hearts that bad rulers will step aside or will change. We in America must change our ways, also. What a wonderful America we would have if our leaders would ask each day, "How can we proclaim God's glory in our decision making?" When we decide to make a serious turn in life, we snatch victory from the Devil. We must change, and we must pray often. God bless each of you in your journey of serving God and promoting peace to all.

Love and peace,

Ruth and Jeff

Challenges

October 1, 2005

Dear Friends,

Challenges, challenges ... Our world and our lives are filled with daily challenges—sicknesses, job concerns, family difficulties, money concerns, and many others. It is how we approach these challenges that makes dealing with them more tolerable.

For almost a month, we have had time to digest the horrors of Hurricane Katrina and, recently, Hurricane Rita. So many people were misplaced, devastated, and left with an uncertain future. But then along came hope, hope from people all over the world. Yes, the Holy Spirit does dwell in all of us, but sometimes it takes a hurricane to awaken that Spirit. So many people—rich, poor, and in between—have had their lives twisted and turned. Let us continue to reach out to people of all races and help them in their times of need. May the Holy Spirit inspire us to serve God by serving others. "Do nothing out of selfish ambition or vain conceit, but in humility consider others better than yourselves" (Philippians 2:3).

As we pray for those who have lost so much, let us ask this question: What have we learned from the hurricane tragedies? Here are some thoughts to ponder:

Know that today is all that God has promised us.

Know that the poor always need our help, not just when disaster hits.

Know that when we only have the shirt on our back, our God is still there.

Know that the Holy Spirit will work in strange ways.

Know that God does not bring bad times to good people but that suffering becomes a way to give glory and praise to God.

Without the bad in our world, how would we know the meaning of true goodness? True goodness comes from the one who is supremely good—our God.

Love and peace,

Ruth and Jeff

Said a Prayer

November 1, 2005

Dear Friends,

We said a prayer the other day that all children would be loved by their parents.

We said a prayer the other day that all people would take time to enjoy God's blessings.

We said a prayer the other day that a cure for diseases would be found and used.

We said a prayer the other day that all people would stop, worship, and give thanks and praise to our God at least once a week.

We said a prayer the other day that all people of all races and beliefs (and unbelief) would be treated as we want to be treated.

We said a prayer the other day that God would take away our weapons and exchange them for hugs.

We said a prayer the other day that we would understand the struggles of the elderly and that we would give them our time and love.

We said a prayer the other day that we would continue to feed and clothe the poor and give them our help.

We said a prayer the other day that God would continue to forgive us and have mercy on us.

We said a prayer the other day that we would slow down and thank God for all the things we take for granted.

We said a prayer the other day that this generation of young people would allow the love of God to occupy their hearts and that they would pass that love onto the next generation.

We said a prayer the other day that government leaders everywhere would pray to God before they acted.

We said a prayer the other day that our TV shows, magazines, and other media would bring clean, wholesome entertainment and information to our lives.

We said a prayer the other day that your heart and soul would be filled with an abundance of God's love and true peace.

Love and peace,

Jeff and Ruthy

Little Jewish Boy

December 1, 2005

Dear Friends,

Long ago, a little Jewish boy was born to parents who were very poor. The cave in which this little one was born attracted many people who were curious to see the child.

This was no ordinary child. He would be the most-talked-about person for years to come. He would be controversial, caring, enlightening, profound, loving, and, at times, hard to understand. Many people would later embrace His teachings. Many would not.

Christmas is the story of exile and birth. Ramadan is a story of fasting and replenishing. Hanukkah is the story of destruction and deliverance. These are three different views of people who were all searching, praying, and trying to live good lives.

Jesus is the One who came for all—Jews, Muslims, Christians, and people of all other beliefs or unbelief. He does not discriminate. The relationship between one person and another is what creates and allows for a relationship with God.

Take time this Christmas to reach outside of your comfort zone of friends. Reach out to someone of a different faith, someone who is poor, someone who is sick, or someone who needs you. Give Jesus Christ the biggest present you can give him this Christmas: the gift of *love* for others.

Have a very merry Christmas and a peaceful New Year,

Ruth and Jeff

Spiritual Ideas

January 1, 2006

Dear Friends,

Each year in the secular world, we sometimes make New Year's resolutions to exercise more, go on a diet, save more money, or change a bad habit. But what about our spiritual resolutions? What about a discussion with God about what he wants next from us in our lives? In our faith journey, we always need to search for new ways to enrich our lives with the fullness of God.

Here are some spiritual ideas we can consider:

- Spend more quiet time with the Lord.
- Pray while you are taking a walk or exercising.
- Instead of watching TV, read the good news of the Lord in a good book or the Bible.
- Make a new friend.
- Help a homebound person on a regular basis.
- Go on a spiritual retreat.
- Take a friend to church.
- Take time to enjoy God's nature—a free gift.

- Mend a broken relationship with a friend or a family member.

We want to wish all of you who receive our monthly "good news" letter the very best in the coming New Year. May it be filled with simple pleasures, may the presence of Jesus be felt in all your struggles and joys, and may God's peace be overflowing in your hearts as you live one day at a time.

Hope never abandons you. You abandon it.

Love and peace,

Ruthy and Jeff

Love

February 1, 2006

Dear Friends,

"What the world needs now is love, sweet love. It's the only thing that there's just too little of … What the world needs now is love, sweet love, no, not just for some, but for everyone."[1]

Those are the words to a song sung by Dionne Warwick many years ago. They still hold true today. With so many people suffering and struggling in our world, we need to continually remind ourselves to love those who are less fortunate.

First Peter 4:8 tells us, "Maintain constant love for one another." With this being the month of Valentine's Day, we can certainly put a different twist on the holiday by opening our hearts to the needy. Our Lord has given us the great command to love Him and also love our neighbor as ourselves. Sometimes, this can be difficult, but if we ask Jesus each day to stand next to us and remember that He

---

[1]   Burt Bacharach and Hal David, "What the World Needs Now" (Sydney: Belinda Music, 1965).

is truly with us, then we are sure to want to please Him by showing our love for others. Mother Teresa says it best: "God does not call us to do great things, but to do small things with great love." We love each of you and pray that God will bring peace in your lives.

Love and peace,

Ruth and Jeff

Today

March 1, 2006

Dear Friends,

A prayer: "Good morning, Lord. What are You up to today? I need You in my heart today. Amen."

What will today bring? That's the big question we ask as we face each new day. Some of our lives are very busy; some are not as busy. What will we do with this gift of today that God so graciously gives us?

Each day should bring about a renewed faith that our God will see us through even in the face of difficulties and obstacles. Faithfulness is a quality that enables a person to continue doing the right thing. Whom will we encounter in our lives today, and how will we spread God's love to those people? Sometimes, our concept of love may come from those we know and may produce an idea of love. But we must come to know and encounter real love—God's love. Then we must become contagious carriers of real love to real people.

Bringing the Holy Spirit into our lives many times during the day will help dissolve our fears, our angers, our hurts, and our feelings of unworthiness. God's unconditional love for us will spread out from us into those we meet.

We all only spend a small time on this earth. Why not spend it with a smile, spreading the good news of Jesus?

Love and peace,

Jeff and Ruthy

No Guarantees

April 1, 2006

Dear Friends,

"And let us run with endurance the race that God has set before us. We do this by keeping our eyes on Jesus, on whom our faith depends from start to finish" (Hebrews 12:1–2).

God does not guarantee a life of luxury and ease. We need to have a constant commitment to hang on and believe in God at all odds, no matter what happens. With the passing of time, each one of us will encounter a difficult challenge. None of us are exempt. Sometimes, we may feel that it is more than we can handle. But when we continue to build a close relationship with God, we can move through these struggles with the assurance that God will never abandon us.

How do we build this relationship? We build our relationship with God one day at a time. Our faith is a work in progress. A faith that gives all our concerns and worries to God is a growing faith. We need to become weak so that God can become strong in us. Let God into your heart each morning by asking Him to walk with you. Focus on God's love throughout each day, and He will spill over into the lives of all those you touch.

When we tell God that we are inadequate to handle certain situations, it is at that moment that our faith in God comes alive. He will never let us down. The very process of living by faith builds strong character.

May the remainder of this Lenten season resurrect in our hearts a passion to serve Christ by serving others. Put our trust and faith in God, and He will abide in us forever.

Love and peace,

Ruth and Jeff

Inner Peace

May 1, 2006

Dear Friends,

Our actions today will affect our future forever. It takes courage to change. Sometimes, it is easier to maintain the status quo.

When Jesus began His ministry, many people were curious about His teachings. In His teaching known as the Sermon on the Mount, Jesus gave us the beatitudes. These are eight attitudes that have great meaning and can change the way we live our lives. Jesus tells us that if we adapt to these beatitudes, then our "reward in heaven is great" (Matthew 5:12).

What is our belief about and what is our behavior concerning the beatitudes?

Reading the beatitudes is a great way to strengthen our faith in Christ. Acting out the beatitudes is a fantastic way to serve our God by serving others. One of my favorite beatitudes is this: "Blessed are the peacemakers, for they shall be called children of God" (Matthew 5:9).

The only way we can experience true peace is to have a deep sense of inner peace. Some of us struggle with our jobs; some, with illness; and others, with getting old and not being able to do as much. Some of us struggle with family relationships; others, with money issues. Still others are searching for a meaningful faith. There is only one way to true peace. It cannot be found in material things, a job, money, or power. Peace can only come to us when we truly open our hearts to the love that Jesus gives us. Once we relinquish our egos and let go of the things of this world, we are on our way to a more peaceful existence.

So, go ahead and have yourself the most peaceful day in your life—a day filled with the love of Jesus Christ.

Love and peace,

Jeff and Ruthy

One Wish

June 1, 2006

Dear Friends,

If you awoke in the morning and could have one dream come true, what would it be? Would you wish for a new job, better health, a more peaceful world, an end to a bad habit, more money, or maybe a mending of ways with a friend or loved one? Well, each day we awake, our dream does come true. It is God's dream for us when we live out His will for us and not what we want. It's a very difficult thing to accept sometimes, living out God's will. It has so many different turns and twists and is sometimes very confusing and hard to understand. But when we let go and let the Spirit guide us, God's plan for us comes shining through our lives. Our ultimate dream is eternal life with God, but before we realize this dream, we must live today's dream—a dream filled with hope that only Jesus can satisfy. The earth will never be our paradise, but it is a marvelous stepping-stone to a life of total peace.

So, as we live our lives and dream our dreams, let us remember that through our struggles and our good times, it is the Lord who is truly guiding us. The question that we must ask ourselves is, are we really ready to give our entire life to God? Can we give our worries and concerns to Him, knowing that He will never fail us?

There are many sayings in life that can help us through tough times, if only we could remember them when we need them. Maybe this little saying says it all: "Life should be more about you and less about me." It is in this saying that Jesus gave His life for all of us. Let us be Christlike by giving of ourselves to others. May Jesus always be in your dreams.

Love and peace,

Jeff and Ruthy

Freedom

July 1, 2006

Dear Friends,

Do we sometimes become complacent about how nice we have it living in the United States? We have freedoms that we don't even think about a regular basis. But what does freedom really mean to us? Try to say this little prayer every morning: "By your death and resurrection, Lord Jesus, you have set us free. You are the Savior of the world."

"It is for freedom that Christ has set us free" (Galatians 5:1).

In his letter to the Galatians, Paul stressed freedom, not rules. Christ freed us from worrying about whether we were doing enough to please God. Being truly free means lovingly serving one another. When we live a life of faith, we free ourselves of the anxieties and concerns of this life and turn to the Spirit for all our guidance. Being truly liberated may help us to understand what Christ really wants for us.

We are free to help the poor and needy.

We are free to smile whenever we want.

We are free to love all people of all races and beliefs or unbelief.

We are free to accept forgiveness from our Lord and others for our sins, and we are free to move on.

We are free to use our God-given conscience to make tough decisions.

Many of the laws of the Old Testament (Mosaic law) were so rigid that the people of that era became bogged down in the laws and forgot how to love one another. Christ came and freed us of these concerns. Do churches today weigh us down with laws and guilt if we don't always follow their teachings?

It is our faith in Jesus Christ which can truly free us of our burdens. Make decisions based on Christ at your side, and remember that He is always loving, caring, and forgiving. Free yourself today by putting on the face of love—the face of Christ.

Love and peace,

Jeff and Ruthy

Marriage:
A Wedding Triangle

There once was a young couple who were truly in love. They decided to be married. They longed for the day when they would be united as one and would start a family.

As plans were made for the wedding, the first thing they did was to invite God into their lives. The three became a triangle of love.

Both the man and the woman decided to relinquish their worries and struggles to God. They did this by showing true respect for one another and always prayerfully requesting God's help with every decision.

Their wedding plans and their wedding day were totally joyous because they put God first in their decisions and in their lives. The couple prayed together daily that they would mold into a loving family, and God granted them their wish.

They became one of the most beautiful, understanding, and loving couples in the sight of God. They will never forget these words: "With God all things are possible" (Mark 10:27).

Blessings

October 1, 2006

Dear Friends,

We have all truly been blessed by God in so many ways. From the beginning of creation, God has poured out His blessings on us, giving us a magnificent world that is beautiful for all to enjoy. When we awake each morning, we are given the gift of a new day, which is certainly a blessing in itself. What we decide to do with God's blessings is up to us. We can certainly give thanks each morning and night for all that God gives us. But we can also share our blessings with others. We can share them by calling a friend, visiting a shut-in, giving to the needy, or being kind to those who may not be kind to us.

We are blessed by God, whether we feel His blessings or not. In the midst of all our struggles, we can still feel God's blessings if only we take the time to realize that God is still with us. Life itself is the greatest blessing that God gives us. And living God's will, not our own, is our challenge each day. By deeply searching our souls and freely opening our hearts to God's touch, we can surely realize that

Jeffrey Faulkner

God truly blessed all of us. May God's blessings be with you every day of your life. How has God blessed you today?

Love and peace,

Jeff and Ruthy

Complicated

November 1, 2006

Dear Friends,

"Complicated. That's what all of our lives are at times." We heard a minister start his sermon with these words several weeks ago. It is true that every day has its complications. We all try to do our very best, one day at a time. But sometimes it becomes overwhelming and very difficult. So what do we do about it? How do we react to these daily struggles? How do we get ourselves to move past a difficult situation?

Probably the best way is to pray about it and then *listen* to God for an answer. The powerful answers that we receive from God can come to us in many wonderful ways. Answers from God can come through a friend, a spouse, or maybe someone we do not even know. God has blessed all of us with the power to help one another—to look after our sisters and brothers. God also answers us through the spoken Word in the Bible. Yes, the Bible can give us guidance for every struggle, problem, or concern we may have. Reading and studying the Bible daily can strengthen our faith immeasurably. The Bible is like the ultimate love story.

Jeffrey Faulkner

So, in our complicated world, we can unwind and untangle any situation with the trust that our God will never abandon us. "Come to me, all of you who are weary and carry heavy burdens, and I will give you rest" (Matthew 11:28). Today, let us all open our hearts to the love that God gives us. Then, we can give that love to others. Yes, it is true that life has its complications and struggles. But it becomes a beautiful world full of endless opportunities to serve God when we listen to His Word and follow His ways. "Be still and know that I am God" (Psalm 46:10).

Love and peace,

Ruthy and Jeff

P.S. Happy Thanksgiving to all.

Materialism and Christmas

December 1, 2006

Dear Friends,

Every year, it seems as if we talk about how commercial and material the Christmas season is. We all buy presents, attend Christmas parties, and decorate our homes, which are nice things to do. Have we ever asked ourselves why Christmas is so commercial and even downright stressful for some people?

The answer is that we choose, as individuals, to make it this way. But God has given us the wonderful gift of free will so we can make a different choice. We can focus on the birth of Jesus, the one who brings us shalom—an inner and deeply heartfelt peace that abides in a caring, giving individual. Christmas is a season of giving, just as Christ gave His life for us. Somewhere in our own communities, there are little ones who will not feel the Christmas touch because they will not be told the real story of Christmas. Their parents will not bring Christ into their lives, for whatever reason. Some of these little ones are poor; some are wealthy. With our prayers and our giving attitude, we can change this situation.

Jeffrey Faulkner

This Christmas, give lots of love to your family and friends, but somehow seek out the poor and bring the Christmas spirit into their lives through Christ. In this day and age, it is easy to get caught up in doing things for ourselves and family. But when that effort becomes a routine of helping the less fortunate, the Christmas spirit lives in our hearts, every day of our lives.

Merry Christmas,

Ruthy and Jeff

Loneliness

January 1, 2007

Dear Friends,

Loneliness. We all feel it and see it at one time or another. We see it in an abandoned child, in sleepless nights, during long days, in a nursing home patient, in a silent phone. These are some of the cries of loneliness—a cry that sometimes goes unheard.

Loneliness is hard to define but can be described in many ways. It exists for an unmarried person who wants companionship, someone who loses a loved one, or a person who loses his or her job. Loneliness is when a friend turns against us or when depression eats at our mind and soul. The most gut-wrenching cry of loneliness in history came not from a prisoner or a widow, but from the cross: "My God, my God, why have you forsaken me" (Matthew 27:46)?

What can we do about this empty feeling? We can all do something wonderful by reaching out to others, especially in January, when many of our spirits are down. Now is the *real season* to reach out to the faces of loneliness. Don't let the spirit of Christmas fall by the wayside. Today, visit a friend, call someone, or write a letter. Tell someone you care by brightening his or her life with your presence.

If you yourself are lonely, then say a simple prayer of faith each day for Christ to give you encouragement.

Let's keep the season of Christmas in our hearts and break out of the winter blues by sharing God's love with one another. We are not called to a life of leisure; we are called to a life of service. Take a friend to lunch, visit a shut-in, help the poor, mend a broken relationship, go to church, surprise a friend with a letter, or help someone you don't know—and turn loneliness into hope.

You are never completely alone when you know and trust in God.

Happy New Year.

Love and peace,

Ruthy and Jeff

Burdens

February 1, 2007

Dear Friends,

As each new day begins, God is there to guide us through whatever we may confront. Our day may be filled with struggles and burdens so difficult that we may cry out to our Lord, "Help me, Lord; this is just too much for me to handle." That is when we can be assured that God will hold us even tighter in the palm of His hand. He knows that we love Him, that we want to trust Him, and that we are trying our best.

How does a mother with all her struggles get through each day? She does it through love, a love that speaks of sacrifices, caring, hard work, and a never-ending concern for her children. How does one move through a sickness or illness that lingers on and on? We tend to look at suffering as something to be avoided at all costs, and, of course, we need to remove suffering from our lives whenever we can. But when we are able to see a larger purpose in our suffering, it becomes a dignified and redemptive suffering. Our struggles and our sufferings can help us grow emotionally, spiritually, and morally.

Jeffrey Faulkner

On those days when we don't even feel like getting out of bed, we need to close our eyes for a moment and picture a brilliant white light. The light is moving toward us and will guide and protect us every step we take in the new day to come. That light is the light that Jesus Christ provides us. It will never go dim.

With our faith, there is hope. And with hope, there is the love of Jesus that will surround us every moment of every day. May God bless you in your struggles, and may He celebrate with you in your joys. Each of you is a precious child of God. He loves you very much, and so do we.

Love and peace,

Ruthy and Jeff

Precious Moment

March 1, 2007

Dear Friends,

How many precious moments do we experience in a day? How many of these wonderful gifts from God do we take the time to really enjoy? With spring approaching and the promise of milder weather, we all become enthused about the upcoming change in the seasons and the moments we will enjoy with the longer daylight.

There are so many precious moments in each one of our lives that we sometimes do not recognize them.

When our grandsons come up to us and give us a hug, we feel like someone has just handed us a million dollars. We carry that hug with us throughout the day as a reminder of God's precious moments, which are truly felt deeply in our hearts.

Look around today and take time to savor the gift of a precious moment. Maybe that moment is quiet time listening to good music with your eyes closed and your worries set free. Maybe the moment comes when you take a simple walk, truly look around, and take

Jeffrey Faulkner

in all the good things the Lord has created for you. Sometimes, a precious moment can be when you are in deep prayer with the Lord and your relationship with Him is deepened. A precious moment may be felt when we have completed a day's work and know that we have done our best, having done that work in God's name.

Precious moments come when we see a child read a book, when we are kind to someone who needs our help, when we listen to a bird sing, when we laugh, or simply when we enjoy the warmth and companionship of another person.

Precious moments are merely reminders of God's kingdom—a kingdom that exists now for all of us. These special moments show us God's continual love for each one of us. What will be the precious moment or moments you experience today? We hope there are many and that you will hold them in your heart forever.

Love and peace,

Ruthy and Jeff

Lent

April 1, 2007

Dear Friends,

What has this season of Lent taught us? It has been a time of
reflection, penance, prayer, and meditation. It has also been a time
to participate in the Lord's death and to let go of the things of this
world that keep our faith from growing. "No one can serve two
masters. He will either hate one or love the other" (Matthew 6:24).
In our world today, it is so very hard to let go of old habits, accept
change, and move on. We like our routine and our comfort zones.
This is why we need prayer and meditation to ask for God's help
and guidance. We hope that Lent has been meaningful for all of
you. We pray that Holy Week will bring all of us closer to God as
we remember the sacrifice of the cross.

When Easter morning arrives, we will again be reminded of the hope
that Christ gave us—the hope of eternal life. The word *Easter*, which
describes the feast of the resurrection of Christ, comes from the word
Eastre, an Anglo-Saxon name for the goddess of spring and fertility.

Our prayer this Easter season is that we all take the hope and love of Jesus Christ and spread it to all people. We will never be able to repay Jesus for all He did for us, but we can certainly imitate Him by showing love and compassion to all.

God bless all of you. Have a joyous Easter and a wonderful spring.

Love and peace,

Ruthy and Jeff

Needs

May 1, 2007

Dear Friends,

Everyone who receives this letter has different needs. As we go through life, our faith may lead us in many different directions. It is by following God's will that we begin to bring our faith to a higher level.

No matter what our needs may be, we all need one another. We are interdependent. We need one another to survive, to grow, and to live as a community of God's children. The student who committed the horrible shootings at Virginia Tech was known to be a loner. He needed help. He needed friends. He had needs, but, to his mind, those needs were never met.

What are your needs? We all need to love, be loved, and be accepted. We all are chasing our wants every day, and our world preaches to us, saying that we will be happy with these things. But what are the deep, desired needs for which our heart is searching every day? We all need peace. We need simplicity, and we desire a loving relationship with God.

Jeffrey Faulkner

So, it is that our life becomes a choice between wants and needs. When we make the right choice, we will come closer to knowing the peace and love that God wants for us.

Love and peace,

Ruthy and Jeff

Choices

June 1, 2007

Dear Friends,

When one awakes very early in the morning, one can hear the cheerful singing of the birds. They bring to us the announcement of a fresh, new day. The birds seem so excited as they continue to sing joyfully until the sun shines its beautiful light upon God's wonderful creation. These little birds then go about their business of providing for their young and maintaining their places of shelter. What God has given these little creatures is so much, and they seem so content and satisfied with what life gives to them.

But what about us? We probably do not begin our days with cheerful singing, but we do have choices. We can start our day in thanks and give praise to our God who gives us this wonderful and glorious new day. Our day will not be without struggles and confusion, but if we can balance our day with prayer, meditation, and quiet time, then we will be able to bring God's peace into our lives.

The next time you awake in the morning, remember the chirping songs of the little birds. They seem to be spreading God's love to all

Jeffrey Faulkner

who hear them. Maybe it is God's reminder to us to be thankful and joyful as we unwrap the gift of a new day. Tell yourself that today you will not give up, that you will stay strong and focused and will persevere. "This is the day the Lord has made, let us rejoice and be glad" (Psalm 118:24).

Be happy and also make someone else happy today.

Love and peace,

Ruthy and Jeff

Truth

July 1, 2007

Dear Friends,

We are all constantly searching for the truth. We are bombarded by political promises, false advertising, products that promise us everything and anything, and a world that tells us that bigger is better and that more equals happiness.

So, what is the real truth? How can we find the truth and be assured that it is the real thing? First of all, it is essential that we have faith and nurture that faith if we are to even understand and bring the truth into our lives.

Consider the following truths taught to us by Jesus Christ.

"I am the vine, you are the branches. He who abides in me and I in him bears much fruit" (John 15:5).

"Love your enemies and pray for those who persecute you" (Matthew 5:44).

Jeffrey Faulkner

"Do not store up for yourselves treasures on earth, but store up for yourselves treasures in heaven" (Matthew 6:19).

"Watch out for false prophets" (Matthew 7:15).

"Do not judge and you will not be judged" (Luke 6:37).

"I am the bread of life. He who comes to me will never go hungry" (John 6:35).

"I am the way and the truth and the life. No one comes to the Father except through me" (John 14:6).

We can read lots of books on self-help, religious themes, how to succeed, and other topics. But when we really want to hear the truth, we only need to follow the teachings of Christ. They will never fail us. If we follow the truths of Christ, then they will bring us a deep inner peace and an amazing amount of spiritual strength. The truth is quite simple—the truth is Jesus Christ.

Love and peace,

Ruthy and Jeff

Mothers

August 1, 2007

Dear Friends,

Several weeks have gone by since our mother passed away. In the days, weeks, months, and years to come, we will always hold her close to our hearts.

The letters we write to you each month are intended to be inspirational and to lift your spirit. Our mom was truly an inspiration to our family and all those many other people whose lives she touched.

Life truly is so very precious, with each new day to be treasured. God is at work every day in our souls with a plan that only He knows and that we must try to follow. Mom has fulfilled God's plan for herself, and now she rests in the peace of His heavenly home.

To each of you who receive this letter, please take just a little time each day to thank God for your loved ones and to pray for those who need our help. Mom did. Be assured that God will never remove you from His heart.

So it was with our mom, who lived a life of devotion to her family, a firm commitment to her faith, and an ever-unceasing willingness to give of herself.

Mom and Dad—we love you, we will miss you, and we will always hold you in our everyday thoughts.

Love and peace,

Jeff and Ruthy

Take a Risk

September 1, 2007

Dear Friends,

It seems that every day our world presents us with so many changes that it just boggles the mind. Changing jobs, changing diets, changing homes, changing stock markets, changing gas prices, and so on—some of these changes can be upsetting, while others can be very rewarding.

But what about our spiritual feelings and our faith? Do we change, or do we just maintain the status quo? Our faith cannot grow unless we change by focusing more of our life on Christ. It is up to us to figure out how much time we really spend in prayer, working with those who need our help, and changing and growing our faith. We are given a wonderful opportunity to change with the coming of each new day. Studying the Bible, volunteering to help others, spending quiet time with the Lord each day—these are just a few ways to grow closer to God.

Jeffrey Faulkner

Mother Teresa often told people to take baby steps with their faith. She said that one will know when one is on the right path to serving God more fully.

Change can be overwhelming to many of us, but changing and growing our faith can be life's most rewarding endeavor. Changing means picking up the cross again and following Christ. Sometimes, this can be a real effort.

But we can find life most rewarding when we take a risk, change our direction, and live life to the fullest. We do this by putting others first in our lives, following our faith, and loving all of our brothers and sisters.

Love and peace,

Ruthy and Jeff

Belief and Action

October 1, 2007

Dear Friends,

Faith is a combination of belief plus action. If you are familiar with the book of James in the Bible, then you know that "faith plus action" is his main message. "Be doers of the word, and not merely hearers who deceive themselves" (James 1:22).

James teaches us that we can find personal wholeness by practicing a religion that is whole and pure—and that religion leads one to devote oneself to those who are in need.

Paul was an early church leader who promoted many people's conversion to Christianity. But it was James who believed that faith and faithful actions could not be separated.

In order to grow our faith, we must be committed to a willingness to adopt the values of God and act on His instructions. How many times each day do we miss a challenge by God to put our faith into action? I know that Ruthy and I struggle with this daily. Our lives are busy with time schedules, places to go, and things to do. Is our focus lost in the shuffle?

Maybe a way to overcome our cluttered lives is to ask God each morning to help us follow His will for us. By asking God for this, we will come into a closer relationship with God and see His presence in our lives. The only thing that keeps us from acting out our faith is our unwillingness to serve the needs of others. But God is patient. He is the great coach who never gives up on His people.

Ruthy and I write these letters because we struggle with faith issues, just like everyone else. But it is in those struggles that God becomes even more real in our lives. May God continue to shower His blessings on all of us as we answer His call to serve others.

Love and peace,

Ruthy and Jeff

Pray

November 1, 2007

Dear Friends,

Prayer can be a great friend of ours if we open our hearts to it throughout our days. Prayer is something we do not have to do, but it is something we should do—and often. The more we pray, the more we stay connected with God and the closer our relationship with Him becomes.

During our day, we should pray in thanksgiving, pray for someone who is sick, pray for a friend, pray for the person in front of us at the grocery store checkout, pray when we hear a siren responding to an emergency, and pray for an enemy. The more we pray, the more we keep the forces of evil from entering into our lives. Prayer awakens our mind, body, and soul to what is really important. "Don't worry about anything: instead pray about everything. Tell God what you need, and thank him for all he has done" (Philippians 4:6).

Talk to God often; it is the most powerful prayer.

Jeffrey Faulkner

Father God, we pray that whoever receives this letter will be abundantly blessed and that your graces will shower their lives.

May the clouds of life turn to sunshine, and may your hearts overflow with love and compassion. You are special in the eyes of God, and He loves you more than you could ever imagine.

When we pray and listen, God will speak to us and will always be there to comfort us. Pray today. Pray now. Prayer is a wonderful journey that leads us to a fantastic destination. We love you, and we will pray for you today.

Love and peace,

Ruthy and Jeff

Light and Christmas

December 1, 2007

Dear Friends,

Even though the days get darker much sooner, December should be a month of light to all of us. There is a light that is always present to us even in a world that turns its back on the light. This light is a gift to each one of us, every single day. And how do we capture that light?

Let us rewind our thoughts to about two thousand years ago, on a quiet night in Bethlehem when a small Jewish boy—Jesus—was born. We celebrate His birth every Christmas and should also celebrate our birth in Christ when we accepted Him as our Savior. We are here to be Christlike in all we do.

This is a most precious time of the year when we, as a people of faith, come together as families to share our love with one another. May that love extend to those who continue to struggle spiritually, economically, and emotionally. The Christmas spirit can be alive in our hearts year-round if we truly put Jesus at the center of our lives. Mother Teresa said, "When we have found Jesus, we have found everything." Try to simplify the season. Imitate Christ by remembering the less fortunate this Christmas. It's the best present we can give to our best friend—Jesus. Even though the world may not be at peace, Ruthy and I pray that each of you will find true peace within your own hearts and capture the light of Jesus.

Merry Christmas,

Ruthy and Jeff

New Beginnings

January 1, 2008

Dear Friends,

May God's peace and love be with each of you every day of the New Year.

What do we want to do differently this year? "Break up your unplowed ground and do not sow among thorns" (Jeremiah 4:3). The more good we do for others, the more riches we sow in the name of God. What percentage of our life is used to produce something of value to God? This is a serious question that demands a serious answer.

We all change from time to time, and sometimes it is hard for us to admit that we need to change. Some of us say, "If I had my life to live over again, I would not change a thing," but that attitude is far too self-serving. We all need to look deep into our own lives and ask God for His mercy. There is great power in confession—to God, ourselves, and others. It is our first step to a New Year's resolution and a new beginning.

Jeffrey Faulkner

Sometimes, we may plan our New Year's resolution and then experience failure. Don't despair. God will always be there to pick you up.

This New Year, let us rely more on the grace of God to guide our path. Stop trying, and begin trusting God more. It is not what we want, but what God wants for us. Simply ask God each day, "What can I do for you today, Lord Jesus?"

May your New Year be filled with the blessings and peace of Jesus.

Love and peace,

Ruthy and Jeff

Perseverance

February 1, 2008

Dear Friends,

It takes a lot of effort to build a strong faith. It does not just happen overnight. Our spiritual life can deteriorate quickly if we give into the temptations of this world. Our faith can also be jolted when things do not go our way.

But God gives us many gifts so that we may fight back during times of difficulty. We can pray, we can take action, and we can trust. And through it all, we will persevere.

"Perseverance must finish its work so that you may be mature and complete, not lacking in anything" (James 1:4).

"Blessed is the person who perseveres under trial, because when he has stood the test, he will receive the crown of life that God has promised to those who love him" (James 1:12).

All of us have received so many blessings in our lives. Sometimes, we take them for granted. During the upcoming Lenten season, we should all take time to reflect on and be thankful for all the special blessings in our lives. Lent is a great time for us to search our souls and renew and grow our faith in God. We can all move our faith in a positive direction by actively helping those who cry out to us.

We can make a difference, we can build our faith, we can love our neighbor, and we will persevere.

Love and peace,

Ruthy and Jeff

Searching

March 1, 2008

Dear Friends,

Today is like most days. It will have its share of peaks and valleys. We will struggle and we will laugh. We will pray, and we will ask God for His mercy and forgiveness.

Some of us will have a better day than others. Some of us will travel many miles, and some of us may not even leave our homes.

So, what is it that we are searching for in our lives of busyness and occasional boredom?

We are "seeking the kingdom of God," and we are seeking and finding it right within our very lives. Even in an evil environment bent on destruction, we can still see the astonishing growth of humanity toward the kingdom of God.

"For the kingdom of God is not a matter of eating and drinking, but of righteousness, peace and joy in the Holy Spirit" (Romans 14:17).

Jeffrey Faulkner

We find the kingdom of God in those who are truly compassionate to others' needs and pain, in the giving of our resources to continue the fight to end world hunger, and in our prayers and quiet times which we share with God.

Seeking the kingdom of God means turning from the ways of the world and following Christ and His example. Our minds become clear, our vision more focused, and our days more filled with the Holy Spirit. The task is not easy, but when we put others first, before ourselves, our lives become more Christlike and the kingdom of God comes closer to us.

Love and peace,

Ruthy and Jeff

Suffering

April 1, 2008

Dear Friends,

The life that God gives to us every day is something that we may take for granted at times. We have received news that Ruth's last treatment for cancer did not work. This journey has been very exhausting and has taxed our faith many times. But Ruthy and I have a tremendous love for our God, and He has blessed us so very, very much in our lives. We have been blessed with such a wonderful, loving family and many friends who care for us as we care for them.

Life is truly the most remarkable gift that God gives to us, and we must always cherish it, every single day—every joy and every struggle. We praise God for the joys, and we praise God for the struggles. What better friend could we ever have—a God who never abandons us?

As you read this, please take just a moment to thank God for someone special in your life. Time is so fleeting that we should always be thankful for this wonderful gift of life that God so freely gives us.

We are very thankful to God for each one of you and hope that you will continue to pray for us, as we will always pray for you.

We are all special children of God.

Love and peace,

Ruthy and Jeff

Answers

May 1, 2008

Dear Friends,

We are all searching for answers. "What will become of me?" "How will we pay for all these bills we have?" "Why is that person so inconsiderate?" "How come I'm not happy?" The questions go on and on. Sometimes, the answers come to us in a prayer. Sometimes, they come from a friend or relative. Sometimes, they come to us in our struggles. And sometimes, our answers come to us in the quietness of the day.

But the real answers come to us when we are willing to trust that God knows what is best for us. When we turn our attention to God, we can be assured that God will answer us. But the answers may not always be what we had in mind. God's will, not mine. This is because we are not in control. God is. He knows what's best for us. When things get real tough, it's time to step back and let God be our guide. We will find the answers when we pray, when we listen to others speaking through God, and when we trust our God. Give yourself to God today.

Jeffrey Faulkner

"Show me your ways, O Lord; teach me your paths. Guide me in your truth and teach me, for you are God my savior, and my hope is in you all day long" (Psalm 25:4–5).

Love and peace,

Ruthy and Jeff

Growing Up

June 1, 2008

Dear Friends,

When I grow up, I want to be more like you, Jesus. Yes, I want to do the things that imitate you. When I grow up, I want to be able to love all people. I want to be able to forgive others who have hurt me and to mend any broken relationships. Yes, Jesus, when I grow up, I want to reach out to the poor, the needy, and the sick. I want to be different like you.

When I grow up, I want to put away the materialism of life and trade it in for a more meaningful life. And, Jesus, when I grow up, I want to set aside time each day for you, to give you thanks and praise.

O Jesus, this growing up is going to be very difficult because it takes so much effort; so much faith, and so much change. And you know I don't always like to change. But, Jesus, I do want to grow up, because the things of this world never seem to bring me lasting happiness. "When I was a child, I talked like a child, I thought like a child, and I reasoned like a child. When I became an adult, I put childish ways behind me" (Corinthians 13:11).

Jeffrey Faulkner

When I grow up, I don't want to be afraid, because you said you'd always stay by my side. And someday, Jesus, I want to be able to do your will, not mine.

And, Jesus, when I grow up, I want to be passionate about something—maybe mission work, spending time with the sick, helping the needy, speaking out for justice for the oppressed. And, Jesus, when I grow up, I want to bring your presence to a world that waits to hear your voice.

Jesus, help me to grow up soon, because we never know how much time we have on this earth. Today is the only gift that we can cherish. Yes, Jesus, help me to grow up today—not tomorrow.

Love and peace,

Ruthy and Jeff

Joy

July 1, 2008

Dear Friends,

Take just a moment to stop what you are doing right now!

First of all, take a deep breath. Are you having a good day or a bad day? Just stop for one moment and smile a big smile!

What is the one thing that is separating you from joy? A promotion? More money? Having a family of your own? Being healed? Mending a broken relationship? What is the answer to the question that will give you joy in your life?

Now answer this: What if that joy never makes its way into your life? Could you ever be happy? If not, then you may be wasting your life away, one day at a time. But wait, you have someone who hears your concerns. He is there at every turn, every valley, every struggle, and every second of your life. Your joy should come in knowing that Christ's Spirit lives within us and is guiding us on the right path.

Jeffrey Faulkner

Your salvation is at stake, and it has nothing to do with the size of your house, the clothes you wear, the job you have, or the stuff you've collected. But your salvation does have a lot to do with the way you treat others, how you focus your life on Christ, and the love that exists in your heart. We may never feel the worldly joys we yearn for, but the joys that await us in our heavenly home are always with us.

It seems that the more we want, the more we become prisoners. We need to unchain ourselves and find contentment in what we have. Even if we lose all of our possessions, even if we were bankrupt or homeless, as long as we have our faith, then we have our salvation.

"The Lord is my shepherd; I shall not want" (Psalm 23:1).

If only we could be content and let God be God. He will take care of us and will bring true joy into our lives. Be content, and God will bring a smile to your face.

Love and peace,

Ruthy and Jeff

Focus

August 1, 2008

Dear Friends,

You hear a lot about "being focused" on what you do. Stay focused and things will be okay. Be focused and the job at hand will be easier.

So, how and when are we supposed to keep focusing on our faith? It's very difficult to continually maintain a consistent spiritual focus. Focusing on and serving Christ never ends.

When we are at work, our ethics should be Christ-centered. When we watch TV or go to the movies, we should make our selection according to a high moral standard. What books we read and what entertainment we enjoy should maintain a focus that keeps Christ at the center of our lives. When we are on vacation, it is a great time to relax and kick back. But it's not time to relax our focus on Christ. We pray at home before we eat, so why not give thanks to God when we eat out?

Actually, everything we do, 24/7, should be focused on Christ, serving and praising Him.

Jeffrey Faulkner

It's a tough battle to stay on track, but it is rewarding. God gives each one of us all the graces we need to live a strong faith-based life. How we accept it is up to us.

As Christ dominates our thoughts, He changes us, molds us, and shapes us until we are ready to live with Him. We have no fear or anger. We think pure thoughts, always trusting. These are lofty goals, but they are highly attainable with a relentless focus on a Christ-filled life. "Set your mind on the things above, not on the things that are on earth" (Colossians 3:2). Wherever you are and whatever you do, turn your thoughts to Christ, and an amazing love will pour out of your heart. Praise be to our God.

Love and peace,

Ruthy and Jeff

Relationships

September 1, 2008

Dear Friends,

Do you ever wonder why we humans cannot seem to get along with one another all the time? Sure, we have some family members and close friends with whom we get along just fine. But what about our enemies, the lazy neighbor, the rude co-worker, the illegal immigrant, people who don't see it our way, arrogant individuals, shady people, and so on? It is easier to be around those who are somewhat like us.

Building true relationships with all people is very difficult for human beings. That's why we need to start with God. By building a true relationship with God, we begin to build lasting and loving relationships with others. If we know that God lives within us and we live within Him, then we will begin to trust that God will always be with us. It's the beginning of a real love affair and lasting relationship. And now, with God in us, we can begin to see that all humans are children of God.

Consider the fact that the gospel writer and apostle Matthew was a dreaded and hated tax collector in his time. But what did Jesus do with him? He asked Matthew to come follow Him, and he did. Jesus calls for sinners to turn from their sins. All of us have a little bit of Matthew in us. We do things that offend others, but we come back to Christ by asking for His forgiveness.

Jesus is about building relationships with people—all people. How we disciple and bring others to Christ is up to us. But we can only do this after we are connected to our loving God.

Try building a relationship with someone different. Be kind, be patient, be understanding. Just being a good listener can ease a lot of pain for someone. Life and love are all about relationships. That's how we grow and learn to respect one another—no matter who we are.

Love and peace,

Ruthy and Jeff

Dreams

October 1, 2008

Dear Friends,

I was almost asleep the other night when a dream came into my mind. All of these wonderful people were gathered around in this most beautiful place. Everyone seemed so content and peaceful. As I looked around, all I could see was a mass of the most fantastic colors filling every inch of space. My ears were consumed with sounds that I have never heard before. They were the most soothing sounds and made me feel as if I were in a trance. As I was standing and looking around and soaking in all the wonderful sights, sounds, and people, I felt a startling warmth come over my body. I could not see what was happening, but I knew that someone's arms had completely surrounded my body. And then I knew that I was in the company of the great Comforter.

We all have dreams and thoughts about being in places that are peaceful and serene. Our only hope is that someday these dreams will come true. By keeping our eyes fixed on the eternal prize, we can make this life a more meaningful one. Days pass by so quickly that

Jeffrey Faulkner

sometimes we forget to stop and look around at all the wonderful sights, sounds, and blessings that we have.

Take time each day just to dream a little about what makes you feel happy. Someday, I know all of our dreams will be fulfilled.

Love and peace,

Ruthy and Jeff

"Then I saw a new heaven and a new earth. ... There will be no more death or mourning or crying or pain, for the old order of things has passed away" (Revelation 21:1,4).

Farewell

November 1, 2008

Dear Friends,

It would be very difficult for me if I did not take one last time to write my monthly letter, this one about Ruthy.

First of all, let me say thank you from the depths of my heart to all of you for your prayers and support over the past five years. The struggle was great for Ruthy, but the reward was even greater. I can tell you that I have felt a lot of pain in these past few days, but I call on the Holy Spirit and He reminds me of all the good there is in this life.

Ruthy and I learned five years ago, when she was diagnosed with cancer, that we needed to take one day at a time and be thankful for each and every moment together. Even as she lay in her bed those last few days—so frail and near death—I was still so grateful to be able to hold the hand of the woman I loved so dearly. I can't hold her hand anymore, but I can hold her within my heart.

Jeffrey Faulkner

Please pray for me and my family these next few months as we move on with our lives. And remember that I will always pray for you.

Love and peace,

Jeff

P.S. Have a peaceful and happy Thanksgiving.

Christmas Dream

December 1, 2008

Dear Friends,

As we approach Christmas Day, I thought it would be nice if you could just sit back, relax, and have a little Christmas dream with me. Picture yourself living two thousand years ago on that first Christmas Day when Christ was born. Maybe you are a wandering shepherd or just someone who noticed the curious light in the sky. Now, imagine walking toward that stable. You see Mary, Joseph, and a tiny newborn baby trying to stay warm in the chill of the evening. Just then, Mary looks over at you and asks you if you would like to come closer and look at the little one. As you stand before the manger, Mary picks up the child and hands Him to you. A deep sense of peace and warmth comes over you as you hold this special baby. *Could this be the Christ child I'm holding in my arms?* Never before have you felt this much love in your heart. This truly is a glorious moment. The Son of God is in your hands. What a Christmas present.

I hope you experience this type of love this Christmas season and all year long. The dream of the Christ child close to us can be real if we open our hearts to His endless love every day of our lives.

Merry Christmas, everyone,

Jeff

New Possibilities

January 1, 2009

Dear Friends,

We now turn the page to a New Year with new challenges and many new possibilities. Remember the beautiful song with the words, "Somewhere over the rainbow, skies are blue, and the dreams that you dare to dream really do come true."

Maybe it is time to open up that rainbow and dare yourself to dream of God opening up new possibilities for you. We are all searching for the sunshine in the blue skies, but, unfortunately, the clouds cover us and bring many struggles and painful experiences. I know that God gives us all the grace we need to sustain us during tough times. But I also know that sometimes we cannot feel that grace during moments of sadness.

That's when we need to look over the rainbow, where God is waiting for us in the bright blue skies. He is always there. But sometimes we make things cloudy.

Jeffrey Faulkner

My wish for all of you this New Year is that not only the dreams that you dare to dream will come true, but also that God will be at the center of those dreams. Rainbows are beautiful images with fantastic colors. Life can also be beautiful if we can open our eyes to God's dream for us. The skies will never be blue all the time, but the sun will shine again when we begin to experience true peace and love in our hearts.

May God shower you with a rainbow of blessings, and may God's dream for you come true.

Love and peace,

Jeff

Imagine

February 1, 2009

Dear Friends,

My imagination swirls round and round at times. I imagine things that probably will never happen. But nevertheless, I imagine them.

If only our imaginations could take us to a world without clutter, disease, sin, pollution, and violence. Imagine, if you can, a world where the food supply is evenly distributed among all people. Imagine that you and I living in a peaceful world that only our Lord knows exactly what it will offer. I also imagine there are pieces of our lives that we would like to see vanish in the wind.

John Lennon of the Beatles wrote a song years ago entitled "Imagine." It says a lot about living in a better world.

Sometimes, my imagination takes me deep within the heart of Jesus, and I embrace His very presence in my life at that moment. It's an awesome feeling, and I wish it would never go away. I know all too well that my Ruthy feels this incredible embrace of our Lord all the time.

Jeffrey Faulkner

My imagination will continue to take me to different places. But I do imagine that I'll have to stop worrying about the past and the future. I imagine I'll have to start living for today—this very moment. I imagine I'll have to change.

What about you?

Love and prayers,

Jeff

Tomorrow

March 1, 2009

Dear Friends,

How many false predictions of end times have come and gone? In the Gospel of Mark 13:32, it reads, "No one knows about that day or hour, not even the angels in heaven, nor the Son, but only the Father." So maybe we should ask ourselves this: If we knew God would come tomorrow, would we live differently than we are living today?

How do we feel about who we are today? Our lives never seem to be on cruise control for very long. There's always that bump in the road that takes us out of our comfort zone. So, what do we do first? We pray and we listen and we follow God's will. Sometimes, that means taking a risk, which makes us nervous. But perched up on our shoulder is the ever-present Holy Spirit to guide us.

Yes, the world will end someday, and life will end for each of us someday. And our success will be measured in terms of eternal rewards, not temporal ones. But what about today? That's the real

Jeffrey Faulkner

issue. We strive to be holy, and we can only do that through prayer, quiet time, and our actions—serving God by serving our neighbors.

We should never fear tomorrow, or else we will miss today. And even if life is difficult for us today, we must remember that real happiness comes to us when we struggle and eventually conquer the problem.

If we can endure the pain of today, then the promise of God will be ours tomorrow—eternal life.

Love and prayers,

Jeff

P.S. A Lenten thought: Learn a new habit or attitude that will stay with you for life.

Darkness and Light

April 1, 2009

Dear Friends,

O how the springtime makes us feel so hopeful of better days to come. It's the spring sunshine that refreshes our minds, our bodies, and our souls. The dark, dreary, wintry days are almost behind us, and now we see God's new season of colors unfold before our very eyes. We again have reason to thank our Lord for the wonders and the beauty of a fresh, new season. But before the brightness of the spring arrived, we had to go through the darkness of winter. Our lives and our struggles reflect this very change in the seasons. It is during the darkness of our lives that we begin to reach way down and find out who we really are. During the dark days of our struggles, we search for answers and sometimes question our God. But trusting God during the darkness becomes our survival kit. Through change and persistent prayer, the light creeps back into our life, and we begin to feel a greater personal freedom to be our true selves.

As we approach Holy Week and the Easter season, let us ask ourselves how we can bring Christ closer to us. Christ gave us His own life on the cross and continues to give Himself to us in so many ways—a

Jeffrey Faulkner

new season, a new baby, a new job, a new attitude. What blessings are new in your life?

As I write this letter, it has been over five months since my Ruthy passed away. I will also cherish the blessings of our thirty-eight years together. But as I moved on, I received a wonderful gift from God—the gift of new friendships. I have new relationships with fantastic individuals whom God has so marvelously placed before me.

Relationships with people—it's God's plan for all of us. We need not walk alone. We need one another. So, as the new flowers and trees blossom this spring, my prayer for all of us is that we grow our relationships with one another and trust that the risen Christ will guide us. If we have a close, intimate relationship with God, then God surely wants us to share that relationship with others. Just as God's beautiful flowers open up with wondrous colors, so, too, should we open up our hearts and lives to others with kindness, generosity, and a loving spirit. May you have a prayerful and reflective Holy Week and a joyous Easter, and may your relationship with God and friends continue to grow and flourish.

Love and prayers,

Jeff

Quiet Time

May 1, 2009

Dear Friends,

The other day, I was watching the sun come up. There were just enough clouds in the sky to make the scene one of brilliant colors. Some of us are morning people, and some are not. But to me, there is nothing more beautiful in nature than the awesome feeling of watching the sunrise. God gives us this fresh new day to start all over again, and the best way to start the new day, besides going to Bob Evans, is to spend a few quiet minutes in prayer to thank God for what He is about to give us.

We take time to nourish our bodies in the morning with breakfast, and we should likewise nourish our souls with a few minutes in the morning, giving thanks to God. By allowing God to come closer to us in the morning, we are setting the foundation for a Christ-focused day.

Jesus had so many demands put on Him during His lifetime, yet He often withdrew to lonely places and prayed. We all have so much noise in our lives that we need and desire this tranquil and isolated time with the Lord. If noise certainly brings stress to our lives, then, certainly, spending quiet time in prayer can bring us peace. Morning time is such a great time to enter deep into the heart of Jesus, tell Him what is on our mind, and really open up to Him.

So, the next time you get a chance to see the sunrise in the morning, just think of it as God's love shining brightly in your heart. Just relax and soak up the wonders of this very beautiful world God has given us.

"Be still and know that I am God" (Psalm 46:10).

Love and peace,

Jeff

Beautiful People

June 1, 2009

Dear Friends,

Sometimes in our lives, we are blessed by the presence of someone who brings us peace and comfort. This person can be so positive and uplifting that he or she seemingly brings us closer to God.

Who are these people in our lives who have brought us to a new level of peace and understanding? On whom can you count when things get out of control and the world seems a mess? Who is the Christlike person (or people) in your life who would do anything to help you?

Maybe it is time to take an inventory of all these fantastic people in our lives who keep giving us hope. Who are these true friends that model and share their experience of Jesus with us? Who is that person who is compassionate toward and always truthful with you? Who are these friends who don't push but lead by example?

As I look back over my life, I see that I have been extremely blessed with many family members and friends who have been so very

Jeffrey Faulkner

inspirational to me. Without my God and these wonderful people, I would have nothing.

Take time to think about these beautiful people in your life, the ones who have helped you with your journey. Be sure to thank them. Say a prayer for them, and thank God for these special angels He gives us every day.

Have a safe and peaceful summer.

Love and prayers,

Jeff

Friends

Dear Friends,

It would be nice to wake up each morning and know exactly what the day will be like. We could better prepare if we knew what hurdles we had to jump. We could avoid a lot of inconvenience in our day if we knew how our day was going to end.

We all know that life does not afford us such an insight into the future. We must prepare the mind, body, and soul for what is about to happen in our lives each day.

One of the best ways to go through each day is to ask a friend for help. We can't do it alone. This friend can give us comfort and assurance on our day's journey. Some days, we may be asked to make sacrifices. Those sacrifices may mean that we must let go or even be willing to die to self-interest or our own ego. This is when we need a friend.

Too many times, we become fearful of situations that never take place in our lives. The anxiety eats at our insides and can cause us all sorts of bodily and spiritual harm. Again, a friend is so valuable in times like this.

When we are hurting or confused, a close friend can be that wonderful person who listens without interrupting and who understands and has a compassionate heart.

So, each night before I go to bed, I call my best friend and thank Him. Yes, thank you, God, for being my best friend.

Love and prayers,

Jeff

Sharing Stories

August 1, 2009

Dear Friends,

Flying home recently from a trip out West, I sat next to a girl who had just graduated from high school. In our conversation, she mentioned that she was getting ready to take a three-month missionary trip with other girls to Africa. She was also sitting there making these little braided bracelets for the children of Africa. She hoped to take two hundred of them to the little ones there.

What a refreshing story about an eighteen-year-old girl, scared to death to go so far away, but ready to do this wonderful thing for little children who have so little. It's a wonderful story because these stories are not told enough. Everyone has a story, but sometimes we just don't take the time to ask. We can learn so much about the fascinating lives that others live when we ask and then take a few minutes to listen.

On my visit out West, I was reunited with a high school friend with whom I had graduated. She and I shared stories that were hilarious, stories that were sad, stories of struggle, and stories of our past. It was good for both of us.

Write a letter to someone you have not seen in a while. E-mail an old college friend. It's so invigorating for the soul to know that others share our same struggles and joys.

Oh, by the way, the name of that high school girl on the plane who was preparing for that missionary trip to Africa was *Faith!*

Wow! How fitting!

Love and peace,

Jeff

Your Smile

September 1, 2009

Dear Friends,

Since I have traveled a lot this past summer, I thought I would share what I saw.

Leaving Port Columbus one *early* Saturday morning, my plane was gliding above the clouds. A lot of you have witnessed this scene many times: clouds so fluffy and with the brilliance of white snow. The sun shone on these clouds and created a color of orange and red that pierced my eyes with indulgent pleasure. The sky was so blue and calm that I began to wonder what lies beyond this magnificent background.

Just think—all this beauty to soak in, and it is entirely free. In the air or on the ground, our world is inundated with sprinkles of beauty around every corner. Again, it is just a matter of stopping and acknowledging this marvelously created landscape.

And as I look at this gorgeous scenery, I am reminded that it pales in comparison to another beauty—and that beauty is you.

Jeffrey Faulkner

Each and every one of you who receives this letter—you are the true beauty of this world. Nothing, absolutely nothing, can replace your personality, your smile, and what you have to offer this world. Nature has a beauty that is just incredible, but nothing is a beautiful as you.

Love and prayers,

Jeff

Sit Down

October 1, 2009

Dear Friends,

Okay, it's letter time. "That's right, it's that time of the month when this guy sends out a letter—and it's supposed to make me feel better. But I've got so much on my plate that I'll probably just read this, say, 'That's nice,' and then move on with the business surrounding all that *stuff* in my life. So hurry up and finish what you've got to say, because I'm a busy person with things to do and places to go."

Okay, I'll try to be short and to the point, but you need to *sit down* for just a minute.

I don't know what you are feeling in your life right now. Are you thrilled about life? Are you hurting about something? Are you sick? Maybe you just don't care anymore. Or maybe life is just so boring and routine that you need a change.

Listen to what Ephesians 5:1 has to say to us. "Be imitators of God, therefore, as dearly loved children, and live a life of love, just as Christ loved us and gave himself up for us."

Jeffrey Faulkner

Now just take one minute and look up to God, tell Him you love Him one more time, and tell Him you love *all* of His children. Tell Him you will love His children by helping them more.

Okay, God, I'm going to really try my best to be kind to all people, because it's really *you that I see in them.* So, God, thanks for this short time we've spent together. I'm already feeling much better!

Love and prayers,

Jeff

Attitude

November 1, 2009

Dear Friends,

The month of November usually brings us dark, dreary days when all the trees become barren. The days grow short; we can become depressed more easily and yearn for those bright, sun-filled days. But we certainly have that one day in November that we cherish. That day is Thanksgiving Day, when families get together for the traditional turkey dinner and an abundance of other foods and desserts.

As I sit here looking out my front window on this cold, dark, miserable, rainy day, I start thinking too much about myself and why there is so much *hurt* in this world. And then I gaze around my room and see the pictures of my four grandsons—and I start to feel guilty for my self-indulgence. God has blessed me with these four beautiful grandsons and so much more in life. My attitude shifts to all the amazing gifts God has given me and the need for me to give my Creator constant praise and thanksgiving.

Jeffrey Faulkner

I know that Thanksgiving Day is a special day for all of us. But we can make every day a day of thanks to God if we just look around at all the blessings we have—family, friends, and faith, and the list goes on.

I know what I'm thankful for each day. I'm thankful for you.

Wow! I think the sun is trying to come out!

Thanks be to God, and love to all,

Jeff

The Christmas Bird

December 1, 2009

Dear Friends,

It was Christmas Eve. There were already three or four inches of white powdery snow laying on the ground. The temperature was a bone-chilling fifteen degrees, and the winds were stirring up and causing it to feel much colder. I decided to take a quick stroll outside before going to bed. I walked outside and immediately looked up to see an abundance of sparkling stars in the sky. I could smell the aroma of fresh wood burning in the neighbors' fireplaces. As I crunched along in the snow, I brought my scarf up to my nose to shield my face from the piercing cold. I took a few more steps and heard the sound of what I thought was a bird. *No bird could possibly endure this weather,* I thought. Just then, I looked down and saw an injured dove lying helplessly in the snow. At once, I rushed home, picked up a box, and went back to retrieve the little bird. Once I had the bird, I took it home and put some straw in a box and placed it in my garage.

As I watched over this little bird, I was reminded of the Christ child's birth and the manger or cave in which He was born over

　　　　　　　　　　　　　　　　　　　　　　　Jeffrey Faulkner

two thousand years ago. This broken little bird also reminded me of the pain and sorrow that our Lord endured for us during His life on earth. That little bird was just fine on Christmas Day, as he was taken in and cared for with love. We are reminded that we must welcome the Christ child into our homes and our hearts again this Christmas by caring for others just as Christ cared for us. The little dove flew away on Christmas Day, and he is a reminder that even though Christ is not physically with us, His Spirit lives on forever within our hearts.

Merry Christmas,

Jeff

Silly Resolution

January 1, 2010

Dear Friends,

This year, I'm not going to make any silly New Year's resolutions. Why should I do something like that when I'll probably just break the resolution in the first few days? I'm not going to get depressed over breaking a New Year's resolution.

But I still want to change some things in my life. So maybe, instead of a resolution, I'll just sit down with God and pray. I'll just have a heart-to-heart talk with Him and let Him decide what is best for me. Then, maybe by praying over this change, I will be moved and guided by the Holy Spirit. By discussing what God wants for me, I believe something meaningful will take place in my life and the lives of others. No, I'm not going to get discouraged over breaking a New Year's resolution, but I am going to ask my best friend for advice. I think I'll stand a much better chance of improving my life if I let God make the decision for me.

Jeffrey Faulkner

I'm not going to wait for someone to invite me to church. I'm just going to go, because the Holy Spirit has already given me a grand invitation.

No, I'm not going to let another day go by without making amends with a family member or friend. There's no way I can face my Lord some day and tell Him that I shun my family and friends.

I'm not waiting for someone to ask me to volunteer. There are too many opportunities for me to help others and spend my time in service to God.

Then there's that neighbor or friend who needs me, but I'm afraid to get involved. I'm not waiting any longer. I'm going to take the plunge. It may save a life or a soul!

Wow! Who needs a resolution to serve God? He's ready with open arms to stand by us on this glorious journey of surprise and wonder, on this mission full of joyous expectations. Who knows, just maybe we will be doing the will of God.

Have a blessed New Year and a fantastic journey.

Love and prayers,

Jeff

Be Still and Listen

February 1, 2010

Dear Friends,

February was named from the Latin term *februum,* which means "purification." In the old Roman calendar, this day of purification was held on February 15. With the cold, damp, and sometimes dreary days of February, the time is ripe for us to examine our own paths and our questionable habits and ask God for His mercy.

But to do this, we must first *listen* to our hearts. We all seem to be people who talk about our busy schedules, and we often forget to give ourselves that peaceful time we need each and every day. Five to ten minutes a day alone with God can do wonders for the soul. God will start changing us from the inside out.

And what about our family and friends? Do we listen to them, or are we so busy talking about ourselves and others that they can't seem to tell us a thing?

My dog, Jax, is a fantastic listener. Whenever I come home, he is so eager to hear from me. He jumps right up onto my lap and can't wait

Jeffrey Faulkner

to find out all the latest news. He never questions my stories and never scolds me for talking too much. Quite honestly, I think that he understands me more than some people do! It's true, my dog may have some bad habits, like doing his business in the wrong places, jumping up on visitors, barking loudly at the mailperson, and so on. But, wow, is he a good listener!

Maybe we all will never be as good a listener as my dog, Jax, but we can sure try by first listening to what God wants for us. Then, by listening to God, we may also be able to hear God's Word speaking to us through others. "Be still and know that I am God" (Psalm 46:10). Listening to others just might help us to stretch our faith.

Note: If you have given to the Haiti Relief Fund, thank you. If you have not given, please consider it. Remember, we are all connected …

Love and prayers, and happy Valentine's Day,

Jeff

Pruned

March 1, 2010

Dear Friends,

"Every branch that bears fruit he prunes, that it may bear more fruit" (John 15:2). We have all heard the story in the Bible about the vine and the branches. Many people have discussed this parable over and over. But do we really believe its true meaning—that more is less? What that means is that we need to cut away those less important priorities and make room for the abundance that comes with God's real plan for us. What is it that is keeping us from the real ministry that God has willed for us? There is pain associated with the pruning of our lives, but the fruits we bear from the pruning become the true joys of living a Christ-filled life. Over the past few months, I have had conversations with several different people, and they expressed their changing (pruning) experiences with me.

A young mother of three was having a difficult time juggling work and raising her children. Then she met an older woman at church. This woman is ministering to this young married mother, who is now feeling better about herself. She is free to bear more fruit.

A retired man was feeling "empty" about his life. He played golf many days a week but was becoming unfulfilled. He bumped into a friend who asked him to volunteer at a local homeless shelter, and he accepted the invitation. He was certainly moved outside of his comfort zone and is now bearing more fruit.

A young married man was becoming dissatisfied with the monthly men's get-together at the local pub. His struggles and pain led him to a Scripture study group once a month, which has not only been rewarding but has also led him to minister to other close friends. And then there was the man I met who had just lost the love of his life. This man felt that God had pruned away every branch of his life. But sure enough, there was a new sprout, and then another and another. After the horrific pain began to subside, all kinds of opportunities to serve God flowed into his life.

What is keeping us from filling our basket with good fruit? Accept the changes (pruning) that God has planned for us and open your heart to the good (fruit) that awaits. When you begin to see the new life sprouting this spring on the trees, be reminded of the new growth that is possible in our lives.

Love and prayers,

Jeff

Retirement

April 1, 2010

Dear Friends,

In a few months, I will be officially retired, although I will still have plenty of odd jobs to do, some lawns to cut, grandsons and daughters and sons-in-law to tend to, volunteer responsibilities, neighbors to help, and who knows what else! Maybe I shouldn't retire!

This leads me to my thought for this letter.

Go into your dreamworld and ask yourself, "What's the one thing I could do in this world to make it a better place?" Don't think too big or you'll get discouraged.

Just find that little niche in your life that you can thrive on and make life better for others. Then ask yourself, "Can I personally stick to this and make it a routine in my life?" We always try to better ourselves in Lent, but the real key to Lent is to carry over those good things we do into our everyday lives.

Jeffrey Faulkner

I'll never forget when my father-in-law, Ed Rutherford, passed away. The minister who was going to do his funeral service visited the family and was asking us questions about Ed. When he asked me what I remembered about Ed, I told him that Ed left his "mark" on life. He cared and was passionate about everything he did.

Did Ed change the world? Yes, through those he touched.

So what about us? Are we leaving our "mark" on life? May God guide all of us in trying to make a difference in the lives of others by following His will.

As we enter this Holy Week, may we remember the sorrows of Christ's death and the sorrows of our lives and know that the joy of Christ's resurrection will lead us to everlasting joy in this life and hereafter.

Shalom,

Jeff

To-Do List

May 1, 2010

Dear Friends,

We all have our to-do lists. They keep us organized and busy. These tiny little reminders outline the things that fill our days. But we just might want to scan that list someday and check for things that really matter. It has been written often that Americans do not pay enough attention to the things that really matter in life. Busyness has consumed us. Our obsession with time has become unhealthy. We need to really get a grasp on our priorities.

God is the one who gives us time, and sometimes we ignore time with God. And what about our health? Is all this busyness good for us physically? The more we become inundated with activities, the more difficult it is to break away from them.

If we have a yearning to find out what truly matters to us, then we need to pause.

Since we are moving into such delightful spring weather, maybe we could take a few minutes each day to listen to our favorite music, lie

Jeffrey Faulkner

on our backs and look at the clouds or the stars, hug someone, laugh out loud, watch the sunset, sing or dance alone, daydream, or just close our eyes and envision only positive thoughts.

So maybe the next time you make out that to-do list, include something on it that truly matters. Just put aside five to ten minutes each day to do something nice for yourself. God says that you really deserve it. May God's love bring a smile to your face.

And may God always be at the top of our to-do lists.

Peace and happiness,

Jeff

Is There Still Hope?

June 1, 2010

Dear Friends,

- We live in a world where one out of every eight people depends on agencies and others for food and necessities.
- Politicians and people we depend on continue to bicker with each other and lie to us.
- Unemployment is still crushing the hopes of many individuals and families.
- Bloodthirsty terrorists continue to threaten our very existence.
- Racism still exists. Is that even possible?!
- Natural disasters bring us together, but our memories are short and we revert back to our old ways.
- Is the stock market really the answer?
- Wars, wars, and more wars—what a waste. When are we going to grow up and learn to just accept and respect the beliefs of others?
- Our inner cities are filled with many young people who have lost hope and continue to turn to the addiction of their choice.

Jeffrey Faulkner

- Many of our young people toss profanity around as if it were an acceptable language. I wonder whom they got that from?
- No more abortions. All of the unborn just voted in favor of a chance on life.
- The family is being constantly redefined, and the new definition is not pretty.
- Why do we keep wanting more and more? Less really is more.
- Chemo labs continue to pump veins with hope.
- Tiny crack babies are born each day, and you know they just want to ask, "Why me?"
- We give a lot—but do we, really?

This is all pretty depressing stuff, but it is real. And another thing that is very real in our lives is hope. God equals hope. Our biggest challenge in life still lies in the future. Because we live in a world of suffering and wickedness, many will lose faith and give up hope. But suffering can be a blessing in disguise if we are willing to accept it. We need to be passionate about something! We need to be strong and let the Holy Spirit control our lives. Don't give up and don't give in, because you will soon witness the great victory. Yes, there is still hope!

Peace, love, and hope to all of you,

Jeff

Traveling

July 1, 2010

Dear Friends,

I was just thinking about traveling down this little road today. It's an adventurous, charming, and sometimes frightening path that leads to all sorts of opportunities. As I wander down this lane, I know I can't do it alone. I'll get lost and frustrated and will want to turn back. So, will you come along with me, protect me, and give me reassurance and support? Will you guide me when I stray off course? I'll need you when I get tired, because sometimes we will go long stretches and the course will be demanding and very wearisome.

As I walk along the road, there are times when the scenery is so overwhelmingly breathtaking that I want to soak in every moment. In the blink of an eye, the road turns treacherous and I become afraid of what lies ahead. You can truly see why I need you with me. I don't know why, but it seems I need you more when the road is rocky.

I don't quite know how long we will travel this road together, so it's best to just take one step at a time and focus on the moment. All in

Jeffrey Faulkner

all, I've enjoyed this walk. But the scenery—it changes so quickly, and I have to adjust to its conditions.

I know one thing for sure: I would not have been able to survive this journey without you by my side. You've been a wonderful companion.

So, if you don't mind, I'd like to continue this little walk, but I insist that you lead the way. You see, I'll follow you because I have all the faith in the world in you. I trust you immensely. And, by the way, I love you dearly.

Your friend,

Jeff

Helping Hands

August 1, 2010

Dear Friends,

How can I help you? Why are you holding back? Sometimes, you seem so distant and out of touch. I want to be able to lend a helping hand, but you have to meet me halfway.

We all have that nagging thing in our lives that seems to keep us from moving forward. I know you pray about it a lot, but sometimes things tend to get worse. Quite frankly, that doesn't make a lot of sense to me. So, if I pray a lot, trust in God, and have mounds of faith in Him, why is it that I still hurt sometimes? What's going on?

All right, let's just back up a little bit. God says the following things to me: Didn't I give you this fantastic gift of life? Look at all the wonderful blessings you have received. And you are absolutely free to choose the way you live. All I ever wanted was for you to be happy and at peace with yourself. Hey, you are the one calling the shots, not me. But I'll give you a piece of advice. Always think of the outcome of your actions before you act. And when you talk it over with me, I'll promise you that you will do just fine. So, what do you say? How about you and I slow down and take a walk together? Let's continue to keep our focus on each other. And just one more thing: No matter how tough things get, please always look up at me once a day and smile. That way, I'll know that you still love me.

Peace,

Jeff

P.S. A thought to ponder: The absence of sin leads to true happiness and holiness.

Taste of Love

September 1, 2010

Dear Friends,

Our love is too small. His love is limitless. What is it about a God that He loves us even in the midst of our faults? How can I change my *small* love and reach out to others? Do we really even have a glimpse of God's endless love for us? As the saying goes, it is easier to love those who love us, but what about that wall of separation that we hold up with some people?

Who of us can actually feel and taste real love?

Ask the man who lost both legs but continues to volunteer his time at a Veteran's hospital. Or what about the little girl who has terminal cancer but inspires her peers with her dazzling artwork? And what about the forty-four-year-old single woman who gave up her comfortable place in New York for a one-room apartment in the slums of Calcutta so she could serve the dying and the poor?

To love is to enter deep within the heart of Jesus. It is also entering deep within the heart of another person.

Jeffrey Faulkner

And so we need to put everything aside for a moment, close our eyes, and fix them on the face of Jesus. Allow yourself to be one with Him. Enter into His soul, His body, and His heart. Let love fill every inch of your being.

Allowing ourselves to get this close to Jesus brings contentment to our lives. And taking that love with us on our life's journey will truly make us more Christlike.

If the only thing we accomplish today is to love each person we face, then truly we are living God's will. So much is written about love, but until we see the face of Jesus in everyone, we will miss sharing in His love. So, I pray: Jesus, let me look into your eyes and feel at peace so that when I look into the eyes of others, I will see your smile and know how to love.

Love to all,

Jeff

Aging

October 1, 2010

Dear Friends,

Another season is arriving. Inevitable changes. Fall's dazzling colors. Twirling leaves. Shorter days. Time is passing. Life is fleeting. We are all changing, and we are all growing older.

Growing older—something we'd rather put off until another day.

On a recent visit to an assisted living care facility, I was visiting an elderly female friend. Another woman who used a wheelchair was in the room with her. I knew this woman and said hi to her. She responded, saying that she could not see me very well, that her hearing was bad, and that she thought she was having a mental breakdown. She told me she wished she could just pass away peacefully, as she had no purpose in life. All I could do was give her a hug and tell her that God loves her—and so do I.

I don't know about you, but I firmly believe that that woman and so many like her have a huge purpose in life. We share in that purpose. That purpose is for us to love them, comfort them, and give them hope. I know that even the elderly whose minds have deteriorated can feel a human touch and are comforted by human love. I truly feel compassion toward these people who sit all day and stare into space. Their lives must be so lonely and depressing.

We can give these elderly children of God a purpose with our kindness and our love. While it is very difficult to see our friends and family members grow old, it can also be very rewarding to give them a sense of purpose by just being with them.

Our love for the sick, the elderly, and the dying is a wonderful way to pay tribute to their lives. The more we show our concern and love for these people, the more we will love ourselves, because someday we will be old ourselves.

Peace to all people,

Jeff

Celebrate

November 1, 2010

Dear Friends,

"Where did I put that list?" "I'm going to be late for my meeting." "The kids are being very unruly today." "I don't have enough time, so don't ask me again." "Get out of my way." "Hey, I thought I told you I can't do that." What a way to start the day! But some of this is, painfully, the way things are.

Even in the most chaotic situation, we can find something to be thankful for if we just take a second to recognize it. Whether we can feel it or not, the Spirit is with us in our deepest depression and our everyday struggles. The next time you reach the boiling point, take a deep breath and rely on the Spirit to guide you. It's a peaceful heart that leads others to peace.

Maybe it sounds odd, but take time to thank God for your struggles and your challenges. When you work your way through them, it is at that moment that your faith in and love for God becomes strengthened.

Jeffrey Faulkner

I just celebrated the second anniversary of Ruthy's passing. That's right—I celebrated. I gave God praise and thanks for all she did for me and my family and for all that she now receives from God in heaven.

Giving God thanks each day for all we have is a wonderful freedom and blessing. The more we put ourselves in a thankful mood, the more pleasant our attitude becomes.

As I have prayed so many times to God, I am so thankful for so much—and especially thankful for you.

Peace, and thanks to God,

Jeff

P.S. Have a blessed Thanksgiving!

A Christmas Shepherd

December 1, 2010

Dear Friends,

There was a chill in the air as the sun began to set. I had a lot of work to do with my flock this night and needed to get started. As the night went on, my fellow shepherd friend noticed a very bright light in the sky that was most intriguing. He was curious about where it came from and asked me if I wanted to go with him to see what was happening near this light. I told him I was very busy, but he persisted. I begrudgingly went along with him. What's the big deal, anyway? Just another bright star cranking up the voltage.

Well, we must have walked about two miles when, all of the sudden, the air got cooler and the light a lot brighter. My body started to quiver. Wow, I wondered what was coming over me. I hoped I wasn't coming down with something. My friend was now getting really excited. He told me of some news, that a baby boy was to be born tonight and he would be king over all people. So now my interest was piqued. As we approached the place where the light was shining, we noticed some other shepherds milling around next to a small stable. Just then, I almost lost my balance as I felt this tremendous sensation inside. I was shaking all over. Getting closer, we could see a tiny baby lying in a bed of straw, with the mother and father close by. As I laid my eyes on this boy, I was overcome with joy and peace. I immediately fell to the ground and gave thanks to my God.

Simplify your Christmas by slowing down and reliving the birth of Christ in your own way. Breathe in the presence of Jesus, and then share His love with others as you enjoy a merry Christmas.

Peace to all people,

Jeff

Flying Insect

January 1, 2011

Dear Friends,

I am a flying insect that flitters into the future. I can see all of 2011 and what it will bring to you and your loved ones. I know it sounds crazy, but you will have to trust me that all will be well this year. I am going to fly right into the teeth of adversity and struggle, as the winds and storms of this challenge are so difficult. As I fly past this messy part of the New Year, I now float into a time of bliss and contentment. A new birth, a new friendship, a new beginning. Wow, I am flying high—so very, very high. But I slow my wings and glide over complacency and, sometimes, the normalcy of life. I need the routine of life every now and then, as it gives me stability.

My wings are beginning to tire now, so I need you to wrap your goodness around my being. I am such a tiny speck in this vast, huge world. Yet, I always want to spread my wings, take a risk, and move ever closer to your plan for me.

It will be a fabulous and exciting New Year if only I can open my heart to all that awaits me.

Jeffrey Faulkner

So, I plan to fly into your world and follow you, the God of all good, the one who loves me unconditionally.

And as I fly high above our world, I look down and see good—the good that you created: I see you.

Peace to your heart, and happy New Year,

Jeff

Happy Ending

February 1, 2011

Dear Friends,

It's the month of love and Valentine's celebration, and there is a new movie showing. The title? *Two People, One Love.* The movie is about two people whose lives were torn apart by the excruciating loss of the loves of their lives. These two people somehow miraculously come together and begin to see one another on a regular basis. They share meals together, talk about their families, pray together, and talk about their spouses and the terrible disease that took their lives much, much too soon.

In a short time, they become a couple and want to be together all the time. They so enjoy learning about each other, sharing their faith, and praying with each other. They are living a dream and never want to awake. It does not take this couple very long until they find out that they are truly connected. They fall in love. They call and text each other often and so desire to be with one another. Their hearts are overflowing with love for one another, the type of love that a lot of people will never have the chance to experience. This couple is now feeling a love that consumes their entire being.

Jeffrey Faulkner

This movie has an incredible ending. There were two wonderful angels always praying for this couple. They ended up being married. By the way, this is a true story. You see, on January 21, 2011, Jeff Faulkner asked Diane Hilliard if she would make him the happiest man alive. He asked her to marry him, and she said yes. They were wed. This movie truly has a happy ending, but it is just the beginning.

Happy dreams and much love,

Jeff and Diane

Happiness

March 1, 2011

Dear Friends,

I don't know about you, but whenever March rolls around, I'm ready to go work outside, run, and just soak up some sunshine. But Mother Nature doesn't always cooperate. The thought of better weather just lifts our spirits and makes us happier people.

Happy people. Isn't that what we all want to be? We all strive for happiness, and Jesus told us that He wants us to be happy.

The trouble is that we all find different avenues to pursue happiness. Some of us find it in a new home, a long vacation, a job change, shopping, technological gadgets, and even more shopping! I do get a lot of satisfaction out some of the above things. But the problem is that it is just not a deep and long-lasting happiness.

Servanthood to others in the name of Jesus—now that's a rich, wonderfully rewarding, and heartfelt happiness. The recipe for true happiness can be found in the beatitudes. It is all so simple, but it takes time and a different mind-set. We need to turn our egos over to God, and then we can free ourselves of the clutter and messiness of this world.

It takes prayer, understanding, and a willingness to put others—not ourselves—first in our lives.

Happiness. I really believe it is found deep within the heart of Jesus. Even though we are sinners, Jesus welcomes us back when we ask for His forgiveness. That surely is a happy thought. So, I guess if we want to find that true happiness, we just need to fill ourselves with the love of Jesus and share that love with everyone, every day.

Happiness and peace,

Jeff and Diane

Mere Existence

April 1, 2011

Dear Friends,

It was difficult to take my eyes off the three fawns playing and running about in my backyard. They did not have a care in the world. Their life was so simple, no clutter, no clocks—just mere existence.

And what about us? Is life complicated for us? Are we all tangled up in a web of busyness? How many times does life tell us to slow down before we are actually forced to do so?

My heart goes out to young people and young families today. They've got so much on their platters. And time passes so quickly; little ones grow up and life goes by in the blink of an eye.

Hey, those fawns in my backyard are now huddled around their mother. Their mood has been quieted by her presence. They are now resting and look so peaceful. They seem to be catching their breaths after a morning of running around. At the end of our day,

Jeffrey Faulkner

as we look back, does it all make sense? Did we have time to even pause and clear our mind?

Lent has always been a wonderful time to ponder our thinking and our purpose, and pray that God will help us live a life that has real meaning.

Those little fawns are now lying down next to their mother. I think they are trying to tell us something.

Peace and quiet,

Jeff and Diane

P.S. Peace comes to a heart that is one with Him.

Eternity

May 1, 2011

Dear Friends,

As a small boy growing up, I had very few cares. Baseball, school, church, neighborhood friends—things were easy. Eternity ... My parents always provided for us—food, clothing, and all the necessities ... eternity. My teen years came along with sports, learning to drive, school studies, and, of course, an occasional date. Eternity ...

Wow—I'm off to college, and who are all these people? What's this type of freedom all about? Staying focused on my faith seems very difficult at this stage of my life. Eternity ... And now I'm married and need to get serious about life because, all of a sudden, I've got two daughters and more responsibilities. Eternity ... I have a pretty good life routine now, as the years pass by. But now my wife has cancer and life takes a big hit. Eternity ... I'm all alone now. How could that be? Wow, who is this new person in my life? Eternity ...

What will happen next? I'm really only assured of the gift of today.

Jeffrey Faulkner

I miss my baseball games, playing marbles, and my mom tucking me into bed at night. Eternity ... from the neighborhood game of flashlight tag to being a senior citizen! It happened all too quickly. But what about eternity? It will last and last and last, forever. We can't even imagine eternity. I remember when, as a small boy, I often told my mom that I just wanted to be a good little boy and go to heaven. I don't know how good I've been, but I have never, ever stopped trying to grow my love for my merciful and wonderful God. In our world, we like to put off thinking about eternity. But in the blink of an eye, it will be here for you and me.

Today is so very precious.

Eternal peace and love,

Jeff and Diane

Small Cross

June 1, 2011

Dear Friends,

While grocery shopping on a rainy day, I noticed a little boy about eight or nine years old who seemed very perplexed. As I was about to pass him, he came up to me and said, "Mister, do you know where the pancake mix is?" I told him to follow me, and I'd show him. On our way to the pancake aisle, I struck up a conversation with him. He told me that his mother sent him to the store to buy just a few things. His mom was not feeling well. He also told me that his father passed away about four months ago. I told him to get whatever else he needed and that I'd give him a ride home since the rain was now coming down very hard.

As I pulled up to his apartment, he asked me to come in and meet his mom. I picked up the groceries, and we headed in. Wow, what a dingy-looking place. There was hardly any furniture—and only one lamp in the front room. Mom looked very feeble, but she nonetheless thanked me for bringing her son home. There are so many people who live this way and in even worse conditions. Yet this mother was so appreciative of all that I did.

Jeffrey Faulkner

What's really strange about this whole story is that this mom thinks I really helped her son. Little does she know that she helped me even more. She made me realize again just how much I really have and don't really need. I mean, how many blue shirts or black shoes does a guy really need? How much stuff does it take to make us happy? Apparently, we'll never have enough stuff.

By the way, just before I left the apartment, the little boy's mother came over to me, reached into her pocket, and gave me a small cross. She said she wanted me to have it because she believes that Christ is our most precious gift. "Has not God chosen those who are poor in the eyes of the world to be rich in faith and inherit the kingdom He promised to those who love Him" (James 2:5)?

Peace and love,

Jeff and Diane

Stories

July 1, 2011

Dear Friends,

Listening equals love.

Oh, if I only would have listened, I would have remembered his first name. And why didn't I listen and pay attention when she gave me directions to her house?

Wow, the art of listening. But I just want to jump in and add a few things so I can set the record straight.

Have you ever been interrupted by a spouse, friend, or someone else who wanted to finish "your" story? That is so irritating. Are my kids really listening to me or just nodding so that I'll stop the rambling?

Sometimes, we just won't let someone finish what they are saying without barging in and adding our words of wisdom!

Good listening involves the surrender of our own self-centered view. Listening produces a genuine love for another and for what that

Jeffrey Faulkner

person has to say. We humble ourselves when we honestly listen to another. Listening is also an unselfish act of giving our full attention to another's thoughts and ideas.

It is only when we listen that we become great storytellers. We can tell stories of life, stories of joy and sadness, stories of love and compassion, stories that unchain us from the past, stories that tell of our faith in God, and stories that share our dreams and our deepest thoughts.

So, go ahead. Don't be afraid to tell your story. You're a precious child of God, and He wants you to share yourself with others. Go ahead and open up—but first be still and listen. Listen to others and, most of all listen, to the voice within you—the voice of God.

Be at peace,

Jeff and Diane

Pray Often

August 1, 2011

Dear Friends,

A little girl approached her mommy and asked her, "Mommy, how often should I pray to God?"

The mother thought for a while and then said to her child, "All the time."

How often do we really take the time to pray to God each day? The Bible says to pray unceasingly to God. Okay, we say our prayers at meals, in the morning, and at the end of the day. But do we pray when we worry, when we fear something, when we are angry, when we are happy, or when we are driving, waiting, thinking, or just doing nothing? Conversations with God on a frequent basis will bring our friendship with God to a new level. It's just like He is sitting next to you.

Some people tell me they don't know how to pray. Just talk to Him. Say what's on your mind, don't hold back, and then listen to the

Spirit work wonders in your life. Sometimes when I pray to God, all I say to Him is, "I am yours; please use me."

We all have different ways to pray, even if it is a moment of silence. I'd like to share with you one of my prayers. Each month, I send out fifty letters to my family and friends. It gives me time to ponder and think about each of you and say a special prayer for you. You all mean so very much to me, and I pray that God will bring peace in your life each day.

Prayer. Embrace it. Talk with God, become intimate with Him, and listen for the Spirit within your heart—and you will be blessed with true peace.

Praying for you,

Jeff and Diane

I Believe

September 1, 2011

Dear Friends,

I believe in the Father, the Son, and the Holy Spirit—the Creator, the love, and the wind in my life.

I believe that all people are precious children of God, including the prisoner, the student, the homeless person, the Muslim, the enemy, and the friend.

I believe that we are all connected with one another and that we just need to discover those connections.

I believe in forgiveness. My Jesus has forgiven me so many, many times. I believe I become free when I forgive and others forgive me.

I believe that we can live together and respect our differences. We learn and grow when we share our stories and lives with each other.

I believe that God has created us to serve Him by serving others. It is our purpose in life. What is it He wants of me today?

I believe that God hears and answers all of our prayers, even if the answer is no.

I believe that we are all called to walk through the pains of suffering. But I also believe that we can experience tremendous growth and strengthened faith when we travel through those difficult times.

I believe that you and I can make a difference. We can do small things to make our communities and world a better place. I believe that we must start making that difference today.

I believe that we must always be sensitive to the needs of the poor. God has blessed us, and we need to pass along those blessings to the needy.

I believe that no matter how bad things get, God still walks with us. Just reach out and hold His hand.

And last, I believe in you, because you are God's special child. He loves you, and so do I.

Love and prayers,

Jeff and Diane

Real Truth

October 1, 2011

Dear Friends,

Do you promise to tell the truth, the whole truth, and nothing but the truth, so help you God? How many people say yes to that and then turn around and lie? We are all searching for the truth, but who can you trust nowadays?

You know the old saying, "The truth hurts." Not only does it hurt, but it also changes us. I really believe that if we want to know the truth, then we must be willing to listen, to change, and then act according to the change.

In some instances, acceptance of the truth can bring us to a very low point in life. We just don't want to accept the change that comes with the truth. But once the truth is embraced, we become free and filled with peace.

The truth is that we must put aside our prejudices. The truth is that we must always forgive. The truth is that we must put aside our pettiness and think about what really matters in life. The truth is that we need our church, our community, and our friends to live life abundantly. The truth is that we all have to accept suffering as a way of life and then trust that God will move us through our pain. The real truth is found in the Bible, and the truth is that we need to read it more often. The truth is that I am a sinner and must daily ask for God's forgiveness. Worldly truths can give us a false sense of security. I will always search out the truth by deepening my faith. I want to know the truth, the whole truth, and nothing but the truth—and with the help of God, I'll find that truth.

Love and peace,

Jeff and Diane

Just Thoughts

November 1, 2011

Dear Friends,

- Strive for holiness.
- Never go to bed angry.
- The sunset puts me at ease.
- Why can't I get a break?
- I want to learn how to pray a deeper prayer.
- How did I get so old so fast?
- Listen.
- Walk, run, just be one with nature.
- Help the poor all the days of your life.
- More for you and less for me.
- Hug someone today.
- If you don't like all four seasons, then try to, as they are another miracle from God.
- Love and suffering teach us more about ourselves and life than we will ever know.
- Forgive and try to forget.
- I really miss my mom and dad.
- My kids and grandkids are so precious to me.

Jeffrey Faulkner

- Jesus, have I told you lately that I love you?
- I long for silence, fresh air, and a clear mind.
- Make this the best Christmas with real meaning.
- Maybe the best prayer is, "Thank you."
- Greed—do we really need more?
- Seek purity always in thought, word, and action.
- Good friends are jewels; families are priceless.

Have a happy and peaceful Thanksgiving,

Jeff and Diane

Christmas Visitors

December 1, 2011

Dear Friends,

It was just another day on the farm for Stephen Finnen. The chores were piling up at his farm home in Brandonville, Maine. Stephen was just a young man of sixteen years who lived with his aunt and uncle. It was six years ago on Christmas night when Stephen's life changed forever. Stephen was a very dedicated, kind, and loving young man. He was a devout Christian, and his heart was always stirring with wonder. On this cold, blustery Christmas Eve night, Stephen was preparing to make a final check on the cattle and sheep barns. All seemed well in the cattle barn, but as Stephen entered the sheep barn, he saw that the door was wide open and the sheep were gone. Running frantically to see where they were, he was astounded when he reached the top of the nearest mountain. The sheep were all huddled around what appeared to be a homeless man and woman. Stephen immediately asked the two strangers if they would come in out of the cold for a hot drink. They obliged. They all tended the sheep back to the barn and headed for the house. Stephen's aunt and uncle insisted that the couple spend the night, as it was bitterly cold.

In the morning, the couple thanked Stephen and his aunt and uncle for the wonderful stay and then started on their way. Then Stephen remembered that he didn't even know the couple's names. So he caught up with them. They told him that their names were Ann and Joseph. Stephen hugged them and started to cry. You see, these were the names of his mom and dad who had died six years ago in a car accident. Stephen believed in his heart that God sent these two homeless people to him as a wonderful remembrance of his beloved mom and dad, Ann and Joseph. Just as these two people came alive again to Stephen, so, too, can the Christ child come alive again to us this Christmas Day.

Merry Christmas,

Jeff and Diane

Change of Identity

January 1, 2012

Dear Friends,

To many people, a new year means a new beginning, a fresh start. "Wipe the chalkboard clean; I'm ready to take on the world!" What is it that we are so enthused about? What motivates our inner being? A new job, a trendy new diet or exercise plan, a new investment, or maybe even a new relationship?

While all these endeavors are noteworthy, can any of them give us a sense of total peace and comfort?

If there is one thing I have learned over the years, it is that nothing the world has to offer can totally satisfy a person. As I start this new year, I have one goal in mind: to be more like Jesus. I want to live the way Christ did. To do this, I may have to change my identity and my direction in life. How can we truly help others, love deeply the poor and sick, and give of our time to others who need us unless our focus is on following Jesus?

Jeffrey Faulkner

We need to stop converting people to *our* way of thinking. We need to accept others, love all, and show them the Jesus in us. Lofty goal? Why not? Just take one day and make a promise to Jesus. Promise Him that you will remember His presence in all you do, think, and say. When you do this, you will be living in total awareness— awareness of yourself, awareness of your life, and, most assuredly, awareness of the Jesus within you. Jesus wants only the best for you and me.

Peace and love to all this New Year,

Jeff and Diane

One with Nature

February 1, 2012

Dear Friends,

There I was, jogging along a narrow path on a cool, crisp winter morning, with the wind bouncing off my face. I was one with nature. I was so blessed to be able to see, hear, run, and feel the wonders of the day.

And then he came at me. This middle-aged man was strolling along the path and coming closer to me. His arms were moving his wheelchair at a pretty fast pace. He started to slow down as he approached me. Then, this man with no legs looked me in the eyes with a smile as wide as Texas and said, "Isn't it a glorious day to be alive? Praise God." And he quickly was off, disappearing around the corner. I was awestruck by his marvelous attitude and, of course, by his broad smile.

How do we handle our setbacks, our sufferings, and our disappointments in life?

Most of the time, we try to take control of our misfortunes. We want to get things back to "normal" as soon as possible. Sometimes, we misread Scripture by focusing on what we must do instead of what God wants to do in us. In due time, God always moves us through our difficult situations and into the light of a new day. That new day comes when we surrender to God and let Him take control.

Here comes that man in the wheelchair again. I stopped to chat with him for a while. He's so upbeat, so positive and such a very pleasant individual. We talked a bit more, and then he left me with this thought: "I may not have legs, but I have a heart, and I've given it all to my Lord." What about us?

Love and peace to all,

Jeff and Diane

A Flower's Journey

March 1, 2012

Dear Friends,

When the flowers begin to make their presence known, it is a sure sign of a new spring. But those flowers are now on a journey and must overcome many obstacles. Early frost can stunt their growth. Too much rain can damage their roots. Drought can wither their natural beauty. And insects and animals can destroy them.

A newborn baby is like a flower. It needs much help in its physical, mental, emotional, and spiritual growth. And we are responsible for nourishing that child so it grows. Just as the flower must move through difficult weather, we must navigate life's challenges. This newborn baby will be exposed to fear, joy, hatred, lies, happy times, faith issues, hurts, sicknesses, proud moments, peer pressure, violence, love, death, and so much more. A lot will be asked of this child along life's journey, even if the child receives little or no guidance.

It is true that someday this little one will have to "unlearn" many things and many bad habits. Just think of our lives and all the things we wish we could change. The answer is that we can change. But we need to make sacrifices. To unlearn a bad habit takes change and willpower and prayer. If we merely keep "repairing" the damage we do to ourselves, then we are essentially going nowhere. But when we stretch our faith, die to our old habits, and replace them with a deeper understanding of life, we begin to flourish.

Each of us must discover for ourselves what path we will follow. And then, come judgment day, each of us will present that path to our Lord. What path are we following today?

Comfort and peace to all,

Jeff and Diane

Why?

April 1, 2012

Dear Friends,

I'm really confused. I've read a lot of spiritual and religious books, and I still ask God these same questions. Why did the world turn out this way, with so much pain, violence, and suffering? Why is it that I have to "die" to this and that to become whole? Why will the people at the bottom be first in the end? And why is it that it seems only the humble acquire true holiness?

I struggle with all of this just like some of you do. It would be so easy to live a carefree, spend-all, do-all kind of life. But that is not what we were created to do. No, God has bigger plans for us. And only by God's grace will we be able to carry out His plan for us. And we will not understand this plan by merely going to church, reading the Bible, or listening to someone else.

It is not until we have reached a situation in our life that we cannot control—a person, an event, a death—that we become powerless. It is only when we bury our ego (and we all have this issue) that we will truly know God and ourselves.

None of us likes to "die" to what we think we are. Letting go is tough stuff. But if we ever want to mature spiritually, we must let go and we must change.

Christ died for all of us, and now we must "die" to our selfish ways. When the ego goes, our souls open up to a life of spontaneous love and letting go. May this be the most awesome day of your life!

Peace and serenity,

Jeff and Diane

The Spirit's Guidance

May 1, 2012

Dear Friends,

It was almost ten years ago. I can remember it well. I made a new friend that day. It was just an ordinary day, but what happened to me that day changed my faith journey forever. Without going into details, I will say that I did something that day that I did not think I was capable of doing. I could not figure out where I got the nerve, knowledge, and composure to pull it off. After it was over, I scratched my head and looked up to the stars. At that moment, I knew it was not me that accomplished what I did that day. It was the Holy Spirit dwelling within me that guided me and gave me the courage to do what I had to do.

I had always prayed to God, Jesus, Mary, and many of the saints. But I had hardly ever mentioned the Holy Spirit.

And now, well, she is my best friend. This third Person of the Holy Trinity is with you and me all the time. When Jesus left this world, He told us we would not be alone. He told us that the Holy Spirit would be with us. We have all been through so much in our lives, and it is the Spirit dwelling within us that soothes our soul, loves us unconditionally, and is always present. How often do we pray to the Holy Spirit or even recognize that the Spirit is alive in us?

I know someone who recently listened to the Holy Spirit and then had the courage to ask two people to come back to Christ—back to church and to a life of faith and hope. What a witness to that person's faith, and what a response to the Spirit's call.

What a gift Jesus left us when He said the Spirit would always be with us. Make the Holy Spirit your best friend. Pray to the Holy Spirit often. You will not be disappointed.

May you live a Spirit-filled life,

Jeff and Diane

Beatitudes

June 1, 2012

Dear Friends,

Okay, we wake up each day. The first thing we do is say our prayers, and we want to do what's pleasing to God all day long. Right?! Wrong …

Oh well, at least we try, don't we?

Being holy and trying to please God 24/7 is our challenge. At work, at play, and during our idle time—are we doing what's pleasing to our God?

If we want to please God, then we will keep His commandments. But if we really want to put a smiley face on God, then we will live and follow the eight beatitudes. Read them, study them, and live them. One at a time. You can follow them if you are a working mom or dad, a single person, a young adult, retired, rich or poor … no matter who you are.

Just look at the eighth beatitude, expressed in Matthew 5:10–12: "Blessed are those who are persecuted because of righteousness, for theirs is the kingdom of heaven." *Blessed* is from the Latin word *beatus,* which means "happy."

I once worked for a company that fired me. I would not cave into their unethical ways, and it cost me my job. Sure, I was sad about it, but I can tell you that it was one of the most *freeing* moments of my life. In this case, persecution equaled happiness and freedom.

When one of my daughters left home for college (which seems so long ago), I told her, "Always ask yourself, 'What am I supposed to be doing at this moment?'" Translated, that means, "Am I doing what is pleasing to God?" There is no vacation time when it comes to pleasing God. When we vacate from His will, we often sin. But O how loving and forgiving He is!

Peer pressure, media, materialism, social status, laziness. These things all detract from doing what is pleasing to God. Here's my formula. Pray often, help others, go to church, read good books and your Bible, be a good parent, love everyone, and do what Jesus asks you to do—follow Him. This is pleasing to God and truly leads to holiness.

Blessings,

Jeff and Diane

Sunday Church

July 1, 2012

Dear Friends,

When I was a young boy growing up in a large family, Sundays always meant getting up early and heading off to church. It was just a way of life. I'm sure I took it all for granted. I just thought all kids went to church on Sunday with their parents. O what a sheltered life I had. It was a good life, but a somewhat sheltered one.

And now, so many years later, I thank my parents for providing me with the opportunity to attend church every Sunday. What a gift—a gift we should all use, no matter what our faith may be.

Who do you know that is missing out on this day of worship and thanksgiving? It's the day when we hear the Word of God and thank Him for all He has given us. It's never easy to ask someone to start going or to come back to church. But at some time or another, we will all probably have the calling to do so. We just need to have the courage to invite others to church.

Jeffrey Faulkner

A church community is vitally important to each one of us. We need each other. We need to learn more about God every day. Your church offers so many wonderful opportunities for you to get involved. Those who think they can do it alone are so very misguided.

Most people, especially young people, have no knowledge that the purpose of their life is to be in union with God. They have been told to go to college, make money, have a family, and die! It's our secular way of living, and it is running wild.

Here's our challenge: Save a soul. Bring someone back to Christ and back to church. It's where we begin, it's where we learn, and it's where we worship and give thanks to our God. Become a person of faith and action seven days a week.

Sex, drugs, and drinking are so rampant today because adults are not promoting church and instilling a good, moral, and faith-filled way of life into their children.

Bring someone back to Christ. Time is fleeting ...

Have a safe Fourth of July.

Blessings,

Jeff and Diane

If

September 1, 2012

Dear Friends,

"If I could just live today all over again." "If I could just have that special moment back." "If I could see her [or see him] just one more time." "I just wish I would have taken more time to ..."

When it comes right down to it, we only have today. Sometimes, the clock is our worst enemy. There never seems to be enough time. How we use each moment of every day is so important.

As I write this letter, I am sitting on our back enclosed patio that overlooks a large wooded hillside. It's very early in the morning and the sun is just peeking through the trees. The grass is covered with dew, birds are chirping and eating from the feeder, several deer appear at the base of the woods, and the air is as fresh as ever.

Time seems to stand still at moments like this. It's a precious moment of peace and serenity, and it is all free! It is a moment like this that brings God, nature, and the human soul together as one. We all need quiet time. Time alone. Time to clear our minds. We need this time to reconnect our spirit with the Spirit of God.

I truly enjoy spending time writing this monthly letter and praying to the Holy Spirit for guidance and inspiration. I pray that you will take a few minutes each day to be at peace with yourself and our Lord.

God is so wanting to spend quiet time with us. How much time do we have?

Peace and quiet,

Jeff and Diane

Lifestyles

October 1, 2012

Dear Friends,

"Many are called, but few are chosen" (Matthew 22:14).

The simple truth is that the Lord is calling you and me. Are we listening? Do we truly follow Christ, or do we do our own thing?

It is all about our lifestyle—the way we treat our bodies, how we approach our beliefs, how we pray, how we socialize, how we help others, what we read, what we watch on our vast array of media devices, and how we think.

If we lead a Christ-centered life, then we will respond to His call. But when we forget that Christ is really in us, we sin. To be blunt, how could we do evil things if Jesus were standing right next to us? Well, the truth is—He is.

Young or old or in between, Jesus is calling us to follow Him—to become holy. It is not a matter of, "Okay, I'll get right with God in a year or two; I'm just too busy right now." "You fool, this night your

Jeffrey Faulkner

life will be taken from you" (Luke 12:20). If you know someone who is not living a Christian life, then reach out to that person. Don't be passive. Time is fleeting, and you are being called by Christ to answer His call to discipleship.

Probably one of the most disheartening things happening in our society today is this: We've twisted, changed, and managed to make our lives suit our needs and not what God wants of us.

We simply justify sinning. The only way out of this hole is to follow Jesus, not the world or the evil in it.

This is not a negative message. It is a message saying that we need to change—and change starts with God and our family. If we put God and others first, then we are changing. When we follow Christ, we die to this world and share in a most wonderful and rewarding journey. It is a journey for which "Many are called, but few are chosen" (Matthew 22:14).

God's peace,

Jeff and Diane

Politics

November 1, 2012

Dear Friends,

Just keep the faith, and in a few more days it will be gone! At least for most of us. I'm speaking of the bombardment of political commercials, if that's what you call them. At any rate, remember that we are blessed with many freedoms in this country, and one of them takes place on November 6. We have freedom of choice. We are free to choose what we consider to be the best available candidate to lead our nation.

But before you vote, be sure to pray. We pray because we want to elect someone who represents good, sound Christian values. Someone who respects life. Someone who is concerned about the needs of the poor and who will be a good steward of our money.

There is another election that takes place every day of our lives. We can elect a life of love and service or a life that is worldly and leads to a dead end.

Jeffrey Faulkner

Our freedom to choose and follow Jesus will last an eternity. We all can choose an attitude of a faith-filled life, or we can ignore it completely. Jesus gives us something that most politicians cannot: He always speaks the truth. He always listens to us. He never lets us down. No one else can say this.

"Come follow me," Jesus said.

Pray often,

Jeff and Diane

The Christmas Shopping List

December 1, 2012

Dear Friends,

My shopping list is complete and my gifts have all been wrapped. To all my friends and family, I've wrapped up the gift of joy in hopes that it will last forever. I've tied a beautiful ribbon around the package of peace, wishing all a comforting year. And over there in that tiny little bag, I filled it with patience and forgiveness in hopes that it will free us completely. And then I filled the stocking with generosity toward all people and a willingness to reach out to the poor.

To my wife, daughters, sons-in-law, grandkids, and extended family, I have wrapped up all my love. I will give it to them every day.

To you, my friends, I have a special box containing a prayer just for you. "You, my friend, are a gift from God. And I will pray for you today, for your health, peace, and happiness. When things get tough, I will pray even more. May you always feel the presence of the Holy Spirit within you each day."

Jeffrey Faulkner

There is one gift we all will receive this Christmas—the gift of Jesus. I'm excited about giving these gifts. And I'm excited about receiving the Christ child in my heart this Christmas Day.

Merry Christmas,

Jeff and Diane

New Year's Thoughts

January 1, 2013

Dear Friends,

The year 2013—what will it bring? What will we give?

Will it be a year of new adventure?

Will it be a year of doubt or faith?

Will it be a year when we change jobs or lifestyles?

Will it be a year wherein every unborn child will be given the opportunity to live just as we live?

Will it be a year of more violence, war, increasing immorality, and natural disasters? (We can only pray it will not be.)

Will it be a year where we read more good books?

Will it be a year when we finally forgive the one we hurt?

Jeffrey Faulkner

Will it be a year when we ask a friend to come back to Christ and church?

Will it be a year when a new friend enters our life?

Will it be a year where we take a few quiet moments every day to thank our Lord for all our blessings?

Will this be the year that we actually sit with the poor instead of writing them a check?

Will this be the year that we say no to more guns, weapons, and bigger armies and learn to be servants of our Lord?

Will this be the year that we accept the shortcomings of our church and move on with our faith?

Will this be the year when we read the Bible more often?

Will this be the year that materialism is no longer a priority?

Will this be the year that we let go of our ego and fill it with the love of Christ and others?

And last, will this be the year that we ask our Lord for nothing except, "Teach me to do what pleases you"?

Peace to all in the New Year,

Jeff and Diane

Letters

February 1, 2013

Dear Friends,

I never envisioned that I would be writing monthly letters for so long a time. This happens to be my hundredth letter! I started years ago, sending them to a few family members and friends, and now I send out sixty letters each month. I truly love doing it. It is my time with the Holy Spirit to search, to learn, and to grow my faith. I will continue writing these letters as long as the Spirit moves me. It has been my ministry. I hope they have given you some inspiration.

God never called you to be anyone other than you. "God has given us the ability to do certain things well" (Romans 12:6).

So, just who are we and how do we get in touch with the gifts we have to offer this world? I have to confess to you that my faith and beliefs were not very strong when I was younger. It has taken me a long time to develop my relationship with Jesus. And I can tell you that I am so grateful to Jesus that He allowed me to live this long and strengthen my faith.

Jeffrey Faulkner

But young people today don't have to be as I was. I can tell you that I have seen and listened to many people in their teens, twenties, and thirties who have already developed a beautiful and solid relationship with Jesus. Believe me, once you start to journey with Jesus, you will not be able to stop. You will want more and more of Him.

We only have so much time on this earth, and we never know when the Lord will call us. Today is a good day to discover your gift. No matter how busy we are, there is always something small we can do for Jesus and our neighbor.

Peace on your journey with Jesus,

Jeff and Diane

Sinner

March 1, 2013

Dear Friends,

Hi. My name is Jeff, and I am a sinner. That's right; I have been sinning since I was a little kid. I am not proud of it one bit. I always try to sin no more, but it happens.

During the season of Lent, you and I have an opportunity to ask our Lord for forgiveness again, just as we do throughout the year. But during Lent, we should take time to prepare ourselves for a better life that focuses on holiness and following Jesus. The more we fill our mind, body, and spirit with His presence, the less time we have for sin.

Developing good prayer habits can become a springboard for a more faith-filled life. All prayer becomes a beautiful relationship with God. And remember, a relationship is a two-way street. We don't get to do all the talking. We need to listen to God, so we will know what His plans are for us. Do we have five minutes a day that we can sit in silence with God? There is so much going on in our lives that sometimes we are afraid of the silence. "Be still and know that

Jeffrey Faulkner

I am God" (Psalm 46:10). Frequent prayer can soothe our worries and bring us closer to God.

We all have our challenges in life. Some are very difficult decisions we must make in order to follow Jesus. When the ego is put aside, our minds become open to what God has planned for us. We become loving, calm, compassionate, and peaceful people who are eager always to serve God by serving others.

"Anyone who fails to love can never know God, because God is love" (1 John 4:7–8).

May we all grow our faith this Lent so we may become more loving and caring to all.

Journey well,

Jeff and Diane

The Right Path

April 1, 2013

Dear Friends,

"I was just twenty-five years old and did not see it coming …" "My spouse never complained about any health issues, and then …" "His job was his life, and then he lost his job and his life much too soon." "I always told God I would give Him more time someday, but someday never happened."

We have just gone through the season of Lent—the season of changes within one's heart and soul. If we have prepared well, we will have less fear of the present and the future. We will also have hope, not hope that all will work out well for us now, but that all will be victorious in the end.

Easter Sunday is the celebration of the greatest gift we could ever receive—eternal life. Christ died for us. So, too, must we die to whatever keeps us from the truth. And once we awake to the truth, the physical death is no enemy to be feared.

Jeffrey Faulkner

So, what's the truth? It's all in the Bible, and it's all about following Jesus.

We need to ask ourselves, "Am I on the right path?" It is a sad commentary that today many people have abandoned church, let their faith decay, and forgotten how to truly love one another.

It is our duty to help others see the truth. May the wonders of the resurrected Lord give us hope and courage to be faithful to His call.

A blessed Easter to all,

Jeff and Diane

Help Others

May 1, 2013

Dear Friends,

If you read John 16:33, you will be reminded that God doesn't promise us freedom from earthly troubles. Maybe that's why our hearts are so troubled at times. Even with the wonderful spring weather ahead, flowers blooming, and longer days, we still have concerns.

How could the leader of a nation (in this case, North Korea) be so hateful toward others? How could someone plant a bomb next to a group of innocent marathon runners? How could we still turn our backs on the poor? How come so many young people are too busy for God in their lives? So much fighting among families ... Shopping malls full of people, and some churches with dwindling numbers ... Quiet time, for some people, has become a lost art ...

With so much troubling one's heart, there is still a light that has never stopped burning: the light of Christ. It flickers for the homeless, the prisoner, the rich, the poor, the nonbeliever, and all of us. Acceptance of this light is not optional if one is to have eternal life with God.

Jeffrey Faulkner

Won't you join me in an effort to get people back to Christ? The numbers are staggering. Among Catholics alone, only 25 percent practice their faith and attend church once a week. Someday, our Lord will ask us how we helped others. And how will we answer Him?

The Light is always on. The Spirit is always within us. Are we ready to stand tall for the one who died for us? Can we take the next step to help someone to a life of following Christ?

Now is the time …

Blessings on your journey,

Jeff and Diane

Spirituality

June 1, 2013

Dear Friends,

How many times a day do we get angry at someone or something? How often do we talk badly of someone? (Be honest on this one—it includes every human being!) How often do we worry about something so much that it makes us sick to the stomach?

Oh my, we humans have so much to learn …

Think about this. When Jesus was born a human being, He came to show us how to live as humans. He did not talk about a religion or church at first. No, He just tried to show us how to be human beings—how to love.

Once we discover how Jesus wants us to live as humans, our anger will subside, our fears will diminish, our hatred will begin to vanish, and our lives will fill up with the peace and love of Christ. It is at this time in our lives that we begin to move in to a spirituality that brings us much closer to God. We see all peoples and all creation as gifts from God. We see the good in others, not the dark side. We

Jeffrey Faulkner

see more benefits to giving than receiving. We walk with Jesus. We pray to Him often. And most of all, we feel peace within our hearts and souls.

Our world is hurting for kind and generous people who can put their own egos aside for the benefit of others.

The world is depending on people like you to fill it with goodness. So, let us model after the great human that Jesus was. Then, and only then, will our faith, religion, and spirituality flourish with love and peace.

May you feel the Holy Spirit within,

Jeff and Diane

Thought for the month: God does not have a plan B for us; He only has *a* plan for us. We just need to follow it.

Pain

July 1, 2013

Dear Friends,

"Please, Mommy, just make it all better. I know you can." This is what the little girl requested of her mother when she fell off her bike and skinned her knees.

Isn't this what we want when we feel pain or sorrow? We want to get through it as quickly as possible. We want instant healing.

But, as we know, it does not always work that way. The process sometimes feels agonizingly long and drawn out. Can't God push the fast-forward button and move me back to being normal?

Diane and I and our families have personally been through a period of pain in our lives that can take a person to the bottom. We lost a dear one. We cannot see or understand at the moment why this is happening. But deep inside our souls, there is a *presence* that is working to heal us and then make us even stronger and more faithful individuals. It is a time to learn, a time to grow, a time to discern, a time to mature, and a time to move forward, doing God's will for us.

Jeffrey Faulkner

None of us are immune to the challenges of life and the minor and major setbacks that come our way. But if we can open our hearts a little more each day to the Light of Christ, we will gain God's strength through our weakness. We come to the realization that we are totally dependent on God. He is in control, not us. Through all of our suffering, we must keep in mind the purpose: God is making us stronger, stronger in our faith and stronger in our love for Him and others.

The little girl just wanted her hurt to *go away* after her fall from her bike. And her mommy wanted to help her so much. The same is true with our God. He wants to help so much. We only need to be open to His healing power and love.

"My strength is made perfect in weakness" (Corinthians 12:9).

—Jeff and Diane

Good News

August 1, 2013

Dear Friends,

Believe it or not, in today's world there is some good news for all of us. For starters, you and I are alive! A fresh new day awaits us. We can't change what happened yesterday, but we can move forward with a positive attitude. How about the young man who recently received his 135th merit badge as an Eagle Scout? Now there is a motivated young man who has an extremely positive attitude for doing good.

We have so many other outstanding individuals that give, give, and give of themselves in order to spread the good news. And that good news is that Jesus lives within each of us. No matter your race, creed, color, or status, He is alive within you. The question is, how will you spread the good news of Jesus today? How will you follow Him?

Here's a challenge. Just for today, say only good things about others. Don't gossip about anyone. It's not easy, but it can be done—and I'm sure you will have a different feeling at the end of the day. It's a feeling that will bring you closer to the heart of Jesus. Could it be the start of a new you and a new me?!

The good news is there. We just have to block out so much from our world that thrives on the negative.

Have a great day. And, by the way, did you hear the good news? Jesus loves you, and so do we.

Peace,

Jeff and Diane

A Matter of Seconds

September 1, 2013

Dear Friends,

We were driving along a country road as the sun was just about to set. Diane was driving as we approached the top of a steep hill. And then it happened ... About a hundred feet before we got to the top of the hill, a truck came flying over the hill in our lane, heading straight for the front of our car. I let out a scream that could be heard in Chicago. Diane did a fantastic job of turning the car into the berm just as the "not too bright" driver flew by us, nearly hitting us head-on.

Life and death ... a matter of seconds. Our hearts pounded, and we were shaking. God was watching over us and the other driver.

This whole incident reminded me that people die every day without "dying to self." "The man who loves his life will lose it, while the man who hates his life in this world will keep it for eternal life" (John 12:25).

Jeffrey Faulkner

If we truly knew what awaited us in heaven, how would we act today? We are called to a life of holiness, not just when it is convenient for us. We are either in it all the way or not.

What do we need to bury in our lives in order to be more Christlike? Do we need to stop wasting, let go of a grudge, stop letting money rule us, put aside our fears and accept suffering when it comes, or rid ourselves of any undesirable addiction? This "dying to self" can only lead to one thing: conversion. And our families, our country, and our world are so in need of conversion.

So the answer for you and me is to die to self—to rid our lives of those things that are unpleasing to our Creator. We must prepare ourselves. You never know who is coming over the hill!

Trusting in God,

Jeff and Diane

Memories

October 1, 2013

Dear Friends,

Five years ago this month, my wife Ruthy passed away. Seven years ago last month, Diane's husband Gary passed away.

Diane and I talk about our former spouses occasionally and share our memories of their lives. While time and love has helped us to heal, there will always be the pain of their loss.

Pain and suffering transformed into joy over a period of time. It's difficult to grasp suffering and joy in the same breath. When you are going through real suffering, at times it feels as if there is no way out. It is draining, disheartening, and sometimes overwhelming. But it does pass.

And one of the best ways to move through this period of pain and suffering is to put Jesus at the center of your life.

Pray more often. Ask Jesus to bless you and your fellow workers before you go to work. Pray before meals. Pray before you exercise.

Jeffrey Faulkner

Pray before your meeting. Pray before you travel. Pray as you take a walk. Pray as you drive. Pray in thanksgiving. Pray as you suffer. Pray as you experience joy. Pray for the person next to you. Pray for inner peace. Pray as you enjoy nature. Pray before you read the Bible. Pray for your families and relatives. Pray for your enemies. Pray for your patron saint. (Do you know who this is?) Pray that we will love one another.

Center your life on and fill your life with Jesus. Diane and I, along with our family, went through a great deal of suffering years ago. We would not be where we are today without our focus on Jesus. We doubted, wondered, prayed, became angry, and were depressed at times, but in the end it was Jesus who was carrying us. Let us pray for each other that we will always have Christ at the center of our lives. Then the suffering and pain can someday be turned into joy.

Praying for you,

Jeff and Diane

Surrender

November 1, 2013

Dear Friends,

In a month that ends with the traditional Thanksgiving Day, maybe it is a good time to pause and reflect on what God has done for us.

We all have some similar and some very different reasons for giving thanks. Giving thanks is something we should continually do every day. But how do we truly show thanks to others and God for what we have in our lives?

We surrender, which doesn't sound like much of a way to give thanks ...

Surrender—something we need to ponder.

Surrender to the hardness of heart that doesn't allow us to forgive. Surrender to the addiction that impedes our way of thinking straight. Surrender to the fears that mess with our minds and make us sick at times.

Surrender to the hate we hold onto and which makes us hurtful. Surrender to a lifestyle that keeps us from attending church, praying often, and seeking to increase our faith. Surrender to a world that tells us we need more. Surrender to a life that will have times of suffering, and learn to grow through them. Surrender your heart and soul to Jesus. What better way to give thanks to others and our loving God than to surrender?

Sometimes, saying "Thank you" is not easy. Surrendering is even more difficult. Give it all to God, and then God will surely say to you, "Thank you."

God's peace to you,

Jeff and Diane

Christmas Snow

December 1, 2013

Dear Friends,

It was getting late. The old man was very tired. He had worked hard that day around his little cabin that was nestled far into the woods. Just before heading to bed, he took his usual stroll outside into the winter breeze. But this night was different. This night he would remember for a long time. This night was Christmas Eve.

As he shuffled along in the woods, feelings of sadness began to pierce his heart. His thoughts turned to our broken world and all the evil that somehow has penetrated God's creation. Why are we so obsessed with violence, wars, corruption, family decay, and a want for more and more? Will it get worse before it gets better? He began to cry as he knelt down on the ground. He, too, was a sinner and was begging Jesus for His forgiveness.

And then he felt a cold, wet sensation on the back of his neck. Looking up to the heavens, he saw a most wonderful sight. It was beginning to snow. The pure white flakes were like fragments of

Jeffrey Faulkner

beautiful crystals sparkling brightly against the light of the full winter moon.

The old man's sorrow immediately began to subside. He felt the cleansing beauty of the snow as a sign of the Lord's forgiveness and love. It was then that he realized the birth of Jesus was like the fresh fallen snow. The baby Jesus would come and make all things new.

Heading back to his little cabin, he looked up into the sky. As the snow dropped gently on his face, he rejoiced and said, "Merry Christmas to you, my Savior. Merry Christmas, Jesus."

Have a blessed Advent and a merry Christmas.

—Jeff and Diane

Persecution

January 1, 2014

Dear Friends,

"Blessed are they who are persecuted for the sake of righteousness, for theirs is the kingdom of heaven" (Matthew 5:10).

If you are thinking of something to focus on in 2014, you may find it to be a daunting task. No one likes to be persecuted, ridiculed, or criticized. But more than ever, we need people today to stand tall for our faith as Christians. If that means rocking the boat or risking it all in the name of the Lord, then so be it. There is a contagious attitude today that tells us to keep quiet about our faith. With so many people starving spiritually, we need to reach out and take a giant step of faith. We need to be proud of our Christian beliefs and spread them to others. You will be surprised at what you can accomplish when you let the Spirit guide you.

But you must also be prepared for resistance and rejection. Being insulted and ridiculed is a sign that we are on the right path. Too many times, we give into the pressures of this world instead of moving forward in the name of Jesus. If you look around this country, you will notice many great evils that are destroying anything that has to do with Jesus, the Bible, and our Christian rights. To live the beatitudes is a huge change and challenge in life. The Word of God is a stumbling block to so many people. Our hearts, minds, and spirits must change in order for our actions to change.

May we each have the strength and courage to stand tall in 2014 to the truth. Learn the truth. Live the truth.

Love to all, and may you journey faithfully in 2014,

Jeff and Diane

Peaceful People

February 1, 2014

Dear Friends,

How many of us can truthfully say that we are at peace with ourselves and our God? We cannot be in control and be at peace. Inner peace is a gift from God, and we need to accept this special gift. Peaceful people are patient with the process to change things.

Sometimes, we become so aggravated with people and situations that we lose our focus. Why do little things upset us so much? Short fuses, bad decisions, and a life without prayer lead to restlessness and aggravation. Peaceful people live in the midst of chaos, through stress, and always with hope.

We live in a world of conflict, hurtful situations, discouraging events, and people who just don't care. Peaceful people move through these tough times with compassion, humility, and a mission in life.

Peace must start with ourselves, our families, and our communities. Peace does not mean that we cave into avoiding the truth and our Christian beliefs. Jesus did not avoid conflict, and neither should

Jeffrey Faulkner

we. Jesus said that He came to divide. We must be willing to accept our challenges in a peaceful manner.

So, is peace the answer to our world's problems? Making peace is a continuous process with families, friends, and enemies.

It is not easy to be at peace with people who hurt us. We feel betrayed and abandoned. Jesus knows how we feel. He remembers it all too well, as He hung on the cross.

But He always forgave others and continues to forgive us. I pray that the peace of Jesus will move us to a closer relationship with God and others.

May peace calm your heart and soul,

Jeff and Diane

My First Love

March 1, 2014

Dear Friends,

We all know how precious life is and what a wonderful gift each of us possesses.

As I approach sixty-six years of occupying space on this planet, I am more keenly aware of the many blessings I have received from God. Wisdom is a remarkable gift itself when used to promote good. What I am about to share with you is my relationship with God. I can tell you quite frankly that it has not always been this way.

First and foremost, I am a sinner. I try so very hard not to sin, because I can't stand to hurt my best friend—Jesus. I love my family so very much—my wife, my children, my grandkids, my brothers and sisters, my extended family, and many other friends and relatives. But my first love is with Jesus, and I will not compromise His teachings with anyone.

I grow closer to Jesus every day through prayer, reading the Bible, reading good books, and trying to love all people. There is also something that brings me so very close to Jesus—and that is the Eucharist. Receiving the body and blood of Jesus on a regular basis has brought me great peace and a strong sense of oneness with Jesus. I know that we all do not share this same exact belief, and that is okay. We all have our faith journey, and we are all aiming for the same eternal prize: heaven.

I don't know why the Lord has let me live so long, just as I don't understand why some die as infants or young people. But what I do know is that Jesus is loving and forgiving. Honestly, we are not guaranteed tomorrow. What will we give back to the Lord today for the gift of life He gives us and for what He gave us by His death on the cross?

Having a strong relationship with Jesus can lead to many loving and intimate relationships with all people.

Love Him, love all,

Jeff and Diane

Worrying

April 1, 2014

Dear Friends,

Some of us spend an awful lot of time tormenting ourselves with worry. Such negative thoughts can be paralyzing. Worrying can be damaging to our mental, physical, and emotional well-being. It seems that we all acquire that troubled look on our faces, even infants, as we battle this thing called "worry" all of our lives. God knows that we have plenty of choices of things to worry about, from children to our jobs, money, growing old, health issues, and on and on …

"Therefore I tell you, do not worry about your life, what you will eat; or about your body, or what you will wear. Life is more than food, and the body more than clothes" (Luke 12:22–23).

It is very difficult to stop worrying, especially when it involves a loved one. But the moment we replace that worrying with positive thoughts, the quicker our worrying subsides.

Pray. Think positive. Act.

Jeffrey Faulkner

I can remember that when I was a small boy in grade school, I just moved through life with a sense of freedom. Mom and Dad took care of me, and I just trusted them completely. Later in life, things became more complicated and I had to put my trust elsewhere—in Jesus. He is always there, and I know He has moved me through some extremely tough times. If only I could trust Him as I did my parents.

We all worry, but let's remember, we all have the heart of Jesus available to hold onto during those anxious periods. Give your worries to Jesus, and He will wrap His arms around you with all His love. After all, you are special to Him.

Prayerfully,

Jeff and Diane

Thought: Replace worry; pray to a saint!

Kind Act

May 1, 2014

Dear Friends,

I was just seventeen years old, and baseball meant so much to me. Just like many boys back then, all I wanted to do was play baseball, talk baseball, watch baseball, and sleep baseball. I remember so many times playing pitch and catch with my dad in our backyard. Fond memories. Dad was never able to see me pitch in a high school game because of his job.

At least, he wasn't able to do so until one late April away game against our rival. I happened to be pitching my best game ever. It was about the fourth inning, and I was on the mound. In between one of the pitches, I noticed this nice-looking man in a tan suit walking toward the field. You guessed it, it was Dad! Wow! What emotions. Dad was here, and I was not going to let him down. Yes, we won and I pitched well, but the memory of Dad taking his time to come see me is etched in my mind forever. Just Dad and me.

When we go out of our way to do a kind act for someone, we may never know the real impact we have on that person.

Jeffrey Faulkner

Time is fleeting. We need to be kind to and considerate of our family and friends. We may never know it, but we just might be making a memory.

Take a look around. Maybe today is the day you will make an impact on someone's life. What you do with your Christlike attitude may just make someone remember you for a long, long time.

Peace,

Jeff and Diane

Awakening

June 1, 2014

Dear Friends,

Looking out the front window of our home one rainy evening, my eyes were fixed on the large maple tree in our yard. The tree has a rather large trunk and two branches sprouting out from each side. This strong, sturdy tree with three main arteries reminded me so much of the Trinity. The trunk, God the Father, our Creator. The branch on one side, Jesus, the Son of God. And the other branch, the Holy Spirit. We can certainly identify with God the Father and God the Son.

But what about the Holy Spirit? Who is this Person to you? Quite simply, the Holy Spirit is God.

One of the greatest needs that our world has today is a spiritual awakening. We are drifting, making our own rules, living for today. The substance of a sound spiritual life is dwindling. Our freedom has been translated into a free-for-all.

Jeffrey Faulkner

So, if ever there was a need for a spiritual renewal, it is now. And who better than the Holy Spirit to touch our lives and lead us to the Father? As long as our ego holds first place in our hearts, we will not be open to the Spirit.

Before Jesus ascended into heaven, He gave us the Holy Spirit. Make the Holy Spirit your best friend. Pray often to the Spirit. Prayerful people become better lovers of life. Open your heart to the Spirit, and you will learn to love others for who they are, not for what you want them to be.

The Holy Spirit doesn't need my ego or yours. He just wants our hearts to pour forth God's love to all.

Now the wind is blowing through the tree in my front yard. The wind of the Spirit is alive and waiting for you and me.

May the Spirit of peace and love be with you always,

Jeff and Diane

Conversion

July 1, 2014

Dear Friends,

In the month of July, as you enjoy your picnics, parades, outdoor activities, and vacations, take time to say a prayer for our nation.

We all have varying opinions, but I believe that we are a nation in dire need of help. Our forefathers laid out a Constitution that made us one nation under God. Sadly, we have drifted and drifted from this way of life. We are truly going through a period of time when the sanctity of the human body is being degraded. We face immodest dress, a lack of morals, murders without reason, killing babies in the womb, making a mockery of marriage, and continuing to turn our backs on the poor and suffering. It is a secular way of thinking, rather than a Christ-filled life, that has brought us to this. Our Judeo-Christian values are being destroyed.

So, where does this leave you and me? If we are to move forward in a spirit of hope, we must fight for the truth, which can only be found by following Jesus. He has never left us, and we certainly must never leave Him by caving into the things of this world. We can still be a happy people; we can still rejoice. But we must be strong and pray often for conversion. We can have all the riches and nice things that money can buy, but they are so short-lived. True happiness is revealed when we have a passion for something worthwhile and live that passion to the fullest.

Be safe, and God bless you,

Jeff and Diane